DUTCHMAN'S PURSUIT

DUTCHMAN'S PURSUIT

David Vaillancour

Rev. date: 04/05/2016

To order additional copies of this book, contact:
Xlibris
800-056-3182
www.Xlibrispublishing.co.uk
Orders@Xlibrispublishing.co.uk
739158

Chapter 1

He felt much better. Once the decision was made it felt as if a huge weight was lifted. It made him apprehensive, slightly worried. It was risky. She might not feel the same way. If she didn't, well, he would have to cross that bridge if or when he came to it.

They were close. They had a close relationship – of sorts. Okay, so it *was* a work relationship, but they spent a lot of time together *after* work too, just the two of them. They shared a lot of personal stuff; well she had anyway. She trusted him, at least he was pretty sure she did. After three years, it was a good foundation.

He knew he was in the 'Friend Zone', but he believed people could move on from there. Why not? He was going to tell her before they left the office today. He thought about what he was going to say and how he would say it for a week. Today was the day; after three years, today was the day.

Later, just before it was time to leave for the day, he went to her office. He was ready; this was it! She was on the phone, very animated, and waved him in. He waited until she was through and had replaced the receiver. She looked at him expectantly.

"Marcie, there's something important I want to tell you. It's . . . ."

"It's the Van Arnsdale job; we got it! We beat all of them and *we* got it. This will *make* us, Dutch, do you realize that?"

"That's great, Marcie, but . . . ."

"Oh my God, I can't believe we really did it!"

He gave a small smile. "This is *your* win. The rest of us helped, but you drove the campaign. Listen, Marcie, there's something I want to tell you . . . ."

"I've got to call Arthur and let him know. He's going to be one happy bunny. If we can pull this off, . . . what am I saying; **when** we pull this off, it'll be the making of us. We'll move right up there with the big guys."

Before he could say anything else, she picked up the phone and called Arthur Teasdale. "Arthur, are you sitting down? Well sit down. We **got** it!"

Marcie spent the next five minutes telling the agency head about her triumph. He waited patiently. When she replaced the receiver, she didn't give him a chance to speak.

"Well that's the next six months shot to hell." She was beaming. Her face had that glow he'd seen a number of times, whenever she shifted into 'Marcie Mode'.

"Marcie, I want to say, ..."

"Save it, Dutch. There'll be plenty of time for congrats **after** we pull this off. I better get alert the troops. I'm going to need everyone here by seven. The clock is ticking as of now." She picked up the phone and began dialling.

He would have no chance to tell her, not when she was in full flow as she was now. She'd landed a major account, the largest their agency had ever secured, and she wouldn't think about anything else from now until they delivered the finished product. She would drive herself and everyone on the team every hour of every day until they were done and nothing, absolutely nothing else, would receive any of her attention.

He felt deflated, like a giant balloon whose skin had just been punctured. He could see the next six months unfolding; long hours, total absorption in the project, personal lives on hold. She wouldn't see or hear or even breathe anything but the Van Arnsdale account. She'd already forgotten, if she ever realized, that he wanted to talk to her; that **he** had something important to say to her.

Why did I bother? What the fuck was I thinking? He got up and turned to leave. He couldn't, he *wouldn't* take another six months. *Even if you could, something else would occupy her mind after that, and it damn sure* **wouldn't** *be me.*

"Just a minute," she said into the receiver. "Come in at seven, will you Dutch? Oh, and pick up doughnuts and bagels?"

He didn't bother to acknowledge her request. At least he'd been ready for this eventuality. He walked back to his cubicle, printed out his letter of resignation, and left it in Arthur Teasdale's in basket. After that he went home and poured himself a stiff drink. He drank half of it and made some calls. The first was to his closest friend, Leroy Nelson out in Oregon; the next was to make reservations for flights to Washington and Portland. After that he finished his drink, had several more, and went to bed.

He was up at seven and wondered, while he brushed his teeth, how Marcie's meeting was going without the donuts and bagels. The phone started ringing at 7:30. He smiled and ignored it. He heard the answer phone record the message to call the office, ASAP **and** immediately. *A little redundant, don't you think?*

He had an Irish coffee and packed his bag. He was careful in his selection of clothing; he wanted carryon luggage only. He wasn't sure how long he'd be gone; if he needed more clothes, he'd buy them as and when. The phone kept ringing every 10 minutes. The messages were increasingly demanding and urgent. At 9:00, he unplugged the phone and erased the messages. His flight was at 1:00 and he was ready by 9:30. He thought about breakfast and opted for a beer instead. Halfway through his second San Miguel, the doorbell rang.

He opened the door and Marcie brushed past him, storming into the living room. "Dutch, what the hell's going on? Arthur told me you submitted your resignation. Why? Why now? You know how important the Van Arnsdale account is. Why are you doing this to me; to us?"

He slowly closed the door. "Good morning, Marcie. How are you this morning?"

"How am I? Confused and pissed off! What the hell is going on, Dutch?"

He walked to the breakfast bar and picked up his half finished beer. Holding it up, he said, "Breakfast mostly. Want one?"

"No, I don't want one! Since when do you have beer for breakfast?"

"Maybe since today. Maybe since always. Maybe since Helmand." He paused. "How would you know what I have for breakfast? Christ, this may be a change from JD for all you know."

She paused, surprised by his tone. There was a hint of, . . . what, anger? "All right, Dutch, what's going on?" She dialled her tone down several notches. "Arthur found your resignation letter in his in tray this morning. What's the problem? Why didn't you talk to me last night?"

He smiled, saddened that she couldn't remember he **had** come to her office to talk, the opportunity lost in the euphoria of the Van Arnsdale win. *The win, always the win; Van Arnsdale, before that Rutgers, before that Samovar, and before that . . . what does it matter?*

"Last night? You didn't seem to have any time; something about Van Arnsdale I think. Things got a little . . . hectic last night, remember?" He took a drink. "There's no problem, Marcie; it's just time to move on. Everything has a cycle. You know, birth, growth, maturity, decline, death; everyone, everything has a life cycle, jobs included."

She looked at him, her lack of understanding tinged with . . . something; disdain maybe? "What *are* you talking about? You into some kind of existential Buddhist philosophy or something? Come on, Dutch, what is it really; a raise, vacation, what?"

He drained his beer and went to the refrigerator for another. She watched him, frowning. In three years, she thought she knew all his moods, the few he ever displayed, but she'd never seen him like this. He was . . . different; cold, deliberate, controlled, and something else she couldn't quite put her finger on. It bothered her, this elusive something else. She prided herself on her ability to read people. *How did I miss this, whatever it is?*

"Sure you don't want one?" he called out. "Breakfast of champions." When she didn't respond, he shrugged and closed the refrigerator door. Popping the cap, he took a drink and returned to the living room. "Where are my manners? Have a seat, Marcie. Would like some breakfast? How about some coffee; juice, toast, eggs and bacon maybe? I have to clean out the fridge anyway and it'll just go to waste if someone doesn't eat it."

She took a deep breath. Her voice was calm, reasoned. He recognized the shift. This was the 'Let's approach this from a different angle' mode. "What you can get me Dutch, is an explanation. Obviously there's a problem. You're angry or unhappy or upset, ormaybe all three. I just want to know what the problem is and what I can do to fix it." She sat down on the sofa and noticed his bag beside the breakfast bar. She looked from the bag to him. "Going somewhere?"

He sat on a stool and took another drink. "Yep; Washington, DC that is, then Portland. After that I'm not sure."

She leaned forward. "Why, Dutch? I don't understand. You're too young for a mid-life crisis."

"I told you, Marcie, it's that point in the cycle. Everything has a life cycle, and this one is complete." He paused and sighed. "I always thought that stuff I read about getting subsumed, losing yourself, getting totally lost was all bullshit, but it isn't. It happens. I didn't see it coming; forest and trees, you know?"

What the hell is he talking about? Has he gone off the deep end? Lost, life cycle, what the hell? "Look Dutch, I need you. **We** need you. You're important to me, to this project. I can't afford to have you walk away now; not now. Come back, at least until Van Arnsdale is done. After that we can talk, relax, take some time. You can take a nice vacation, company expense, anywhere you like. When you come back, we can reassess; see where we go from there."

The more she said, the sadder it made him. *How could I have been so stupid? There's no way in hell she has any feelings for me. None. Never did, never will. She isn't worried about me, just what I mean to the project. Don't think she has feelings for **anybody**. Sometimes people you work will never be more that the people you work with. Damn boy, you were really whippin' a dead horse. Lucky you **didn't** say anything.*

He looked at her and smiled. "No we wouldn't, but it's okay, Marcie. You just don't get it and I get you don't get it. It's done; I'm done. It is what it is. Nothing going to change you, or me."

"Me? Was it something *I* did? What, when? Just tell me. We need you, Dutch. I don't want to do this project without you."

His smile broadened. "But you will. You want to do this project more than anything, with *or* without me. You don't need me. You need **somebody** and you'll find someone, Marcie. Hell, you found me. There are lots of people out there who can do what I do."

"But not everyone can work with me the way you do. This project is too important to break in somebody new. There isn't the time. You know me, I know you. We work so well together. Come on, Dutch, you love what you do. Stop this nonsense and come back to the office."

He slowly shook his head. "You don't know me at all. That's the problem." He paused. "The project, the project, always the project. You know what? Fuck the project!"

She drew back, physically recoiling. She'd never heard him swear. She'd never seen him anything but calm, reasoned, and unflappable. At this moment, she wasn't sure who this man was.

"All right, Dutch," she said getting up. "I'm sorry you feel like that. I'm sorry things have to end this way." She paused. Looking at him, she felt a number of conflicting emotions, some of which she didn't understand. "Good luck."

She turned and walked toward the door. As she opened it she heard him say, "Thanks, Marcie. Good bye." She was back on the street and into a cab without any recollection of how she got there. Dutch stared at the door for a long time after she left. There was certain finality in the sound of it closing.

"He won't change his mind, Arthur." Marcie was pacing back and forth in front of his desk. "I just saw him. He said some really strange things, but the bottom line is, he won't change his mind. He says he's going to Portland by way of DC, but I don't know why."

"Did you ask him?"

"All he said was everything has a life cycle. What does that mean?"

"But did you ask him why he's going there, to Washington and Portland?"

"No."

"Why not?"

"I want to know why he's leaving, not where he's going."

Teasdale sighed. "I was afraid this would happen."

Marcie was surprised. "You knew this was going to happen? Why didn't you say something? Why didn't you tell me?"

"I stay out of people's personal lives, unless they invite me to interfere, of course."

"Personal lives? This is business, Arthur."

"No, it isn't, Marcie."

"I don't understand."

"I know. Dutch is in love with you, Marcie. He has been for a couple of years now. Even I could see it."

She leaned back in the chair, shocked. *In love with me? Dutch? How was that even possible? He never said anything; he never did anything. He never let me know how he felt. Dutch Yancy? That's ridiculous!* "Arthur, you can't be serious! Dutch Yancy, in **love** with me? Where did you get an idea like that?"

"It was obvious, Marcie; well not you, of course. You're get so completely immersed in your projects, you have a hard time seeing anything else. That's what makes you so good at what you do. Unfortunately, it doesn't do much for your personal life but, as I said, I stay out of people's personal lives."

She was having trouble getting to grips with the idea of Dutch being in love with her. *How is that possible? How did I not know? Why do I think it's impossible?*

"Arthur, what am I going to do? I need him. I need him on this project. I need him on all my projects. He's special."

"What's so special about him?"

She paused. *Well, what **is** so special about Dutch? Was he so technically proficient that no one else could do what he did? No, of course not. Then what?* Teasdale waited patiently. Finally she said, "He's innovative Arthur, and that's what we're all about. He comes up with solutions that other people don't see, even when it has nothing to do with his area. And . . ."

"And?"

"And he can work with me. I get, . . . ratty sometimes, especially when things aren't going well. I can be impatient and short tempered. I've almost lost several people because of it. At one time or another, everybody on my team has threatened to quit; everyone except Dutch. Somehow he just ignores it and gets me to work through the problem, even smoothes feathers I may have ruffled." She paused. "You know, I don't think I ever even apologized to him for that. I never saw the need. I never thought it was necessary." She paused, longer this time. "Now you see why I need him. He's special."

"Why do you think he was able to work with you and be so patient with you when others wanted to quit? I already told you what made him so special, and it had nothing to do with his technical proficiency or personal skills."

"But, . . . I never thought of Dutch in that way."

"Do you ever think of *anyone* in that way?"

She shook her head. "Not since college." She frowned. "Arthur. What am I going to do? I need Dutch, I want him back but . . ."

"You don't have feelings for him, at least not *that* kind."

"I, . . . I don't know. I never thought, . . . I don't know."

"If you had any emotional attachment, you'd know. I'm afraid I can't help you. I'm not sure how you can resolve this, or even if it can be resolved in any way that would keep him here."

She sat for a few minutes in silence, then got up.

"What are you going to do?"

"I don't know, Arthur. Talk to him. I don't know what I'm going to say, but I have to talk to him."

She left the office and caught a cab. She missed him at his apartment. She also missed him at the airport. Later on she realised – she missed him.

Chapter 2

This was his second year at the Annual Portland Swap Meet. The first year he did better than he expected, probably better than he should have in spite of the fact that he'd brought the wrong merchandise. The majority of his stock was frying pan clocks. They were cast iron frying pans with the clock face on the bottom of the pan. They were novel and looked good on the kitchen wall. Best of all, they were easy to make.

The first year he sold about three quarters of the pan clocks he'd brought with him. By contrast, he sold *all* of the burl clocks and people kept asking for them, even after he'd sold out and had only his display models left. He gave people his card, so they could contact him after the show and order by mail. It was a waste of time and cards. Each burl clock was unique and people wanted to see what they were buying.

The burls were cut from Red Alder, Black Cottonwood, White Oak, or Maple trees. The wood was hard to work and the burls even harder to find. When each clocks was completed, they made a beautiful, decorative piece for the wall. The wood pattern was different, distinct, and unique; no two were alike. When you owned one, it was the only one of it's kind and there would never be another like it.

Friday, the first day of the show, was always slow. He took his time setting up and putting up the banner that read, ***IT'S ABOUT TIME***. When he was done, he settled down with a book. He had a selection of

Robert Parker paperbacks, several of the Jesse Stone series and some Spenser's. By late afternoon he'd sold three clocks and finished the first paperback.

He was just returning with coffee from the refreshment stand when he noticed two figures in front of his stall. For a second he thought there was something vaguely familiar about the woman, then dismissed the idea and walked past them to enter from the side.

He didn't pay any more attention to the pair. There were always more lookers than buyers. He was about to sit down, when a familiar voice caused him to stop dead in his tracks.

"Dutch? Is that you?"

He would have known Marcie Watsons' voice anyplace, even after three years. He straightened up and turned to face her.

"Hello, Marcie. It's been a long time."

She looked the same – but different. Her hair was shorter, a little more makeup, slight frown creases in her forehead. She looked a little . . . harder, but still gorgeous. A flood of memories and emotion washed over him.

"Oh my God, it **is** you! You're here!" She was having trouble accepting the coincidence.

"Everybody's got to be someplace. What brings you to Portland?"

"Client conference at the hotel. We don't fly out until Sunday so we thought we'd kill some time and come over here to look around. And here **you** are!"

She's buying herself time to figure out what to say. Seen it before – I was there, Marcie, remember? "You're looking well. How is everything? How's Arthur?" He spoke to her but looked at the man with her. Medium height, medium build, regular features, watching Marcie's every move. *One of Marcie's poodles.*

"Thank you. Oh Dutch, this is Sebastian Brakewell. He's one of the team on the account. Seb, this is Dutch Yancy. Dutch used to work with me."

They shook hands. *Average but you'll do pal. Just don't try to outshine Marcie.*

"It's about time," she read from the banner. "Is that what you're doing now?"

"Yep, that's me."

She tried to hide her surprise and something else. *You feelin' sorry for me, Marcie?* She hesitated, embarrassed, and unsure what to say next. "The wood in the clocks is very unusual, really lovely. Where does it come from?"

Nice recovery, girl! "The wood or the clocks?"

"Both."

"The wood is from the forests south of here. The clocks are mine; I make them."

"You make them? Really?"

"Wouldn't try to fool you, Marcie. Everything you see, I made."

She was at a loss. She couldn't imagine anything more unlikely than Dutch Yancy making clocks. It was so, . . . so, . . . ludicrously funny! If someone had told her, she wouldn't have believed it. "I'm just, . . . surprised. How long have you . . . ."

"Three years, ever since I came out here."

"I remember you saying you were coming here, but I didn't know this was where you settled. No one did. You didn't stay in touch with anyone. No forwarding address, so no one knew where you'd gone. Do you work locally, here in Portland? What is it you do?"

He knew from the way she was speaking that she was struggling. He pointed at the banner. "That's me, my company. I make and sell clocks. I have a place about 45 minutes southeast of here."

"You do this; for a living?" Her disbelief was evident

"For a living."

She didn't know what to say. He had never seen her at such a loss for something to say before. For some perverse reason, he was enjoying her discomfort. *This is childish. Oh hell, this is fun!*

Finally he broke the silence. "So how is Arthur?"

"Oh he's fine, fine. Cutting back, but he still comes in every day and he's still involved with everything. So what is it you do? How do you actually make these clocks?"

"Once I find the right tree, on with a burl, I cut the burl and bring it back to my shop. I cut and sand and finish the wood and then I assemble the clock. The frying pan clocks, I just drill and assemble."

"Where did you learn to do all this?"

"Oh, you know us craftsmen; born with the gift."

"It's just so . . ."

"Unexpected? Surprising? I'm a surprising kinda guy."

"Well they're lovely, really lovely." Her tone sounded genuine.

"Thank you."

"I don't want to keep you, but I'd love a chance to catch up. We're here until Sunday morning. How about dinner at the hotel tonight?"

"Afraid I can't. The show is open until ten, so I won't finish until at least eleven or later."

"What about a drink then, after you close?"

"I'd like to, but I've got a long day tomorrow. The show opens at ten and closes at eleven at night."

"Breakfast then, how about breakfast? Come on Dutch, it's been three years. You're not trying to avoid me, are you?"

Damn right I am, sweetheart, like bubonic plague! She's just going to keep after me, like a dog with a bone.

"All right, but it'll have to be early; seven o'clock. I need to be here before nine."

She smiled. "Wonderful! I'll see you in the coffee shop at seven. I'm looking forward to it. It's lovely to see you, Dutch." She still knew how to use that dazzling smile; that hadn't changed.

"Yeah, you too Marcie."

Shit! Shit, shit, shit, shit, shit! Of all the exhibitions in all the world, . . .

He walked into the coffee shop just before seven and saw her sitting at a booth in the rear. As he got closer, he could see she must have been up for a while. Her makeup was flatteringly flawless. It certainly wasn't slapped on a hurry. She wore a dark green sweater, tight fitting and low cut.

Damn girl, what's this is aid of? I'm no prospective client. This is **breakfast***, not dinner before we hit a few clubs!*

"Good morning," she said brightly. She had been watching him ever since he came in the door. "I didn't think to ask; are you staying here in the hotel?"

"No. Have you ordered?"

"Not yet. I waited for you. I think it's too early to order beer, though." She smiled.

"Never when I'm working. Put's the customers off."

The waitress came over and they ordered; toast and coffee for her, bacon, eggs, hash browns, toast and coffee for him.

She looked at him, trying to adjust to the change. In New York, the pale complexioned Dutch wore loafers, suit and a tie. This tanned Dutch wore boots, plaid shirt, and blue jeans; worn looking jeans at that. He was relaxed, laid back, and . . . something else. Comfortable? Self-assured?

"So," she started, "what are you, some kind of lumberjack, crashing through the woods, saw on your shoulder, looking for a tree to kill?"

He looked for condescension in her tone but she was just being cute. "Not quite. I only take a burl and only from dead trees."

"Oh." She paused and seemed unsure of what to say next. He waited. *Come on, Marcie. Not like you to hesitate.*

"I have to confess, I'm having trouble getting my head around this, . . . this Dutch, model two point oh."

"No mystery to it; long as I have to earn a living, I might as well do something I like."

"I thought you liked what you *were* doing."

"I always like what I'm doing, until I don't or until it has run its course and it's time to move on to whatever the next thing is. This is the next thing."

"Is that why you came out here when you left; so you could do this?"

He paused before replying. "No really. I didn't have any idea what was next when I came out here,."

"I would have thought you'd . . . ."

"Find a job doing what I did at Teasdale?" he asked, interrupting her.

"Well, . . . yes."

"When I told you everything had a life cycle, I wasn't talk about New York and Teasdale; I meant the job, the city, what I was, everything."

"So what did you do? Tell me, please? I'd like to know."

"It's not important, really. I'm here, doing what I do."

"Please, Dutch."

"Okay. I went to D.C. There was someplace I had to visit to pay my respects to some old friends." His visit had been to Arlington National Cemetery. "After that, I flew out here and stayed with a friend for a while. He made clocks for a hobby. I got interested and tried my hand at it. I liked it so I found a vacant barn in a little town, built a workshop and a place to live, and I started making clocks.

"I started with the easy ones, the frying pan clocks. They're simple and foolproof. I sold them to gift shops and at swap meets. People seemed to like 'em. After a while I got bored. The pan clocks weren't much of a challenge. One day I saw a piece of burl and the pattern was amazing. I started experimenting, figured out how to work the wood and turn it into a clock. The rest is what you see." Breakfast arrived and they continued to talk as they ate.

"And you make a living at it?"

He nodded. "Oh yeah. I don't make as much as I did at Teasdale, but I don't need as much as I did in New York. I live in my workshop and I make enough to keep me and Sasha in beans and bacon."

"Sasha? You're married?" There was surprise in her voice and a cold feeling in her body.

He smiled. "I'd love it but Sasha and I aren't compatible. Besides, I think there's a law against it; or maybe it's against the natural order of things for a man to marry his dog."

"Sasha is your dog?" She couldn't hide the relief she felt.

He held his finger to his lips. "Ssshhhhh! She doesn't know that," he whispered.

"What kind of dog is she?" Marcie whispered back.

"A Czech Wolfdog."

"A what?"

"A Czechoslovakian Wolfdog. She's a cross between a German Shepherd and a Carpathian wolf."

"A wolf? Is that safe?"

He shrugged. "She hasn't attacked me yet."

"But a wolf?"

"Wolf**dog**. There's a difference. Sasha's fine. She's very protective."

"So it's just you and Sasha then?"

"So far. It works out pretty well. Sasha's a great listener; lousy conversationalist, but a great listener; gives me someone to talk to at night who never disagrees with me."

She smiled, feeling more relaxed. This was like the old days. Sometimes after work over a drink they would chat and it was always easy, like now. She missed that. She hadn't realized how much she had missed him.

"How about you?" he asked. "Arthur make you a partner yet?"

"Probably this year. We're on track for the best year we've ever had and I think he'll make me a partner by the end of the year, barring any unforeseen problems."

"I thought after Van Arnsdale, you'd make partner for sure."

"He might have, but we struggled, and it didn't go as smoothly as it could have. I think it actually set me back. It took me a while to get back on track, but everything is okay now." She didn't mention the reason. She didn't have to.

"Congratulations in advance, then. It's what you always wanted. You deserved it long before now. I never knew anyone as dedicated or hardworking as you."

"Thanks, Dutch." She paused. "You know, it wasn't the same after you left."

"I'm sure everything was just fine without me. You know what they say about the indispensible man; take a bucket of water; stick your hand in it up to the wrist. The hole you leave when you pull it out, is the measure you'll be missed."

"That may be true of some people, Dutch, but you were missed - for a long time." She was looking at him, her expression serious.

"Come on, Watson, don't get maudlin. That's not you."

"You might be surprised."

He knew he needed to go before the conversation turned any more serious or tread on ground he'd rather not walk. He looked at his watch. "Well, before I am, I better be getting along. Lots to do before I open. Today is the busiest of the three days. It'll slow down again tomorrow, but today will be busy – I hope."

"I'd like to stop and buy a clock."

"Tell you what; stop by and I'll *give* you one, any one you like."

"I couldn't do that."

"Of course you can; I insist. Consider it a reunion gift or a Happy Promotion gift. Come by any time." He slid out of the booth. "I really have to go. I'll get the cheque on the way out. See you later."

She did stop. He gave her a clock. They talked for a minute. She left.

Chapter 3

Arthur Teasdale had only been in his office 10 minutes when Marcie rang and asked to see him. He was surprised she looked so troubled.

"Problem on the trip?"

"No. The client is happy and gave us the go ahead. Sebastian seems all right. I think he'll work out, if he stops being so deferential and starts telling me what *he* thinks."

"Stop intimidating him."

"I don't intimidate!"

"Sure you do. Everyone is intimidated by you at first. You are a very strong personality, Marcie. If the client is happy and Sebastian has possibilities, why do you look so out of sorts?" She was frowning. "Something happen in Portland?"

"I saw him."

"Him?"

"Dutch."

"Dutch? Really?" He leaned forward, interested. "Where? How? How is he? What's he doing out there?"

"I ran into him at a sort of arts and crafts show. He had a booth, selling clocks. That's what he does, apparently. He lives in a barn with a wolf and he makes clocks!"

The image caused him to raise his eyebrows. "Sounds like the opening sentence of a hell of a book or maybe a country and western song. He lives with a **wolf**?"

"That's what he told me."

"Interesting. How did he seem?"

"He seemed, . . . I don't know; relaxed, laid back."

"Happy?"

"I don't know. I think he **thinks** he is."

"What kind of clocks?"

"What?"

"The clocks; what kind of clocks are they?"

"Some are made out of frying pans and some are made out of wood. The wooden ones are really beautiful. He gave me one. I'm going to put it up in my office."

"Is that where he lives, Portland?"

"I don't think so. He said something about a small town."

"Sounds like you two had quite a conversation."

"We talked over breakfast."

"How does he look?"

"All right."

"Just all right?"

"Okay, he looks good. He was dressed like a cowboy, but he looked good."

"Sounds like life in the Pacific Northwest agrees with him."

"He **can't** be happy, running around dressed like a . . . a . . . . one of the Village People. He lives in a barn with a wolf and makes **clocks**! **Clocks**, for Christ sake!!"

"It sounds like **you're** the one who's not happy."

"He's better than that, Arthur. He's got all that talent and he's wasting it."

"And you think he should be here, using his talent."

"Well, . . . yes," she admitted grudgingly.

"Seems he's found other talents. How do you think **he** feels about it?"

Marcie Watson posed a special problem for Arthur Teasdale. She was brilliant, but her brilliance was hampered by an emotional volatility that could be counter productive. When Dutch Yancy left so abruptly, it knocked her for a loop. He had never seen anything have such a negative effect on her. It knocked her off her game so badly, that at one point he seriously considered replacing her. She managed to pull herself together, but it worried Teasdale and he was concerned again now, and for the same reason.

"I don't know how he feels."

"Did you ask him?"

"No."

"Why not?"

"I don't know."

"That's at least four times you've said I don't know." She said nothing. "The first thing you should do is admit *why* you want him back here." She started to speak but he raised his hand to stop her. "The *real* reason. If it's because he's wasting his life and his talent, that's fine. I don't believe that for a minute; I think it's an excuse. You have to figure out whether you still love him."

"*Still* love him?!"

"Yes, *still* love him. Come now Marcie; why should you care if he makes clocks in Oregon? The man's been gone for three years! If you don't love him, let it go; let him get on with his life, and you get on with yours. If you *do* love him, and perhaps you do, then tell him. Find out if he loves you. If he does, the two of you sit down and figure out what you're going to do about it. Don't leave it hanging. Settle this, once and for all, or it will keep eating at you."

She didn't say anything, just sat looking at him with an unblinking stare. He waited patiently. When a single tear started to trickle down her cheek, he wordlessly reached into his drawer and handed her a tissue.

"Thank you." She daubed at her eyes. "Do you really think I'm in love with him, Arthur?"

"Probably; possibly; maybe."

"You never said anything."

"You never asked and I don't meddle."

"How did I not know? How do I know now?"

"You're single minded and driven. It's what makes you so good at what you do. But you lock out everything else. When was the last time you were in love, or at least thought you were?"

"I don't know – college."

"Go out much?"

"I go out," she said defensively.

"What sort of men?"

"I don't know, . . . men."

"How do you feel about these men? What are they, friends, lovers; ever get emotionally involved with any of them?"

"This is starting to feel like a therapy session."

He looked at her for a moment. "You're right, I apologise. You asked me what I thought and I told you. What you do now is up to you. If you don't love Dutch, let it go; let *him* go."

"This is such a mess. ***I'm*** such a mess!"

Back in her office, she sat staring out the window at nothing. *How can Arthur think he can see what I can't? What makes him think I'm in love with that stupid Dutchman? If he **really** loved me, he would have said something. Why didn't he tell me when he was leaving? Why didn't he say something now? What if he had told me then? What would I have done? Nothing, that's what! If I don't know how I feel now, I sure as hell didn't know then.*

When he left, could I have stopped him leaving? I couldn't say I loved him if I didn't. Maybe I could have skirted around it, told him we could take it slow and see. Why didn't I do something when I saw him this time? God he looked great! But he's a different Dutch. He's not the Dutch that left three years ago. Did I love that Dutch? Could I love this Dutch? Forget did I ever, what about right now? Can I see myself with this Dutch, doing all those cheesy things people think are so romantic?

She thought about that for a long time and decided she could.

Chapter 4

It was a great show for him. He came back to Sholalla with almost no merchandise. He'd run out of burl clocks again. He wasn't sure what he should do for next year. He could make more, but only if he made fewer pan clocks. But pan clocks were his bread and butter. They sold year round and there was an ongoing market for them. If he **had** to have problems, these were the kind he wanted.

On the other hand, Marcie Watson was the kind of problem he did **not** want. It took him the better part of a year, a lot of clocks, and Sasha to get over Marcie. He still thought about her off and on during his second year in Sholalla, then hardly at all in the past year. Her unexpected appearance in Portland put paid to that! *At least she's back in New York and thank God for small mercies.*

Over the next few days he thought a lot about Marcie Watson. He hadn't examined how he felt about her and what happened for a long time. He didn't want to feel *anything* about her. It took him three years to get where he was now and he liked the place he was in. But there she was, on his mind. He could still remember the day he first met her, all the subsequent long hours, the hard work. He remembered the meetings; how frustrated, annoyed, impatient she could get, and how he learned to calm her down and get her back on track. He remembered the times when they sat in the office late at night, just the two of them, drinking and talking. He remembered how he came to care for her and how that grew into something else. He also remembered that last day, the realization that she didn't feel any of the things he did, or anything at all of a romantic nature, as far as he was concerned. In fact, she had no feelings for him at all. He was just somebody she worked with, period. Any regret she felt at his leaving had to do with his work skills and his contribution to her project's success (which was also her success), and nothing to do with him as a person. Three years on there was no reason to think anything had changed. He was becoming angry and morose, much like he'd been when he first came to Sholalla. It took a lot of clocks to get out of that state; that and Sasha.

He'd only been in Sholalla about six months, angry and upset at himself because he was. He still wasn't the most outgoing, friendly person in town, but at least he was halfway civil. One morning, Pat Stallings, the local vet showed up on his doorstep, uninvited. There was no pet rescue and re-homing organization in town – there was just Pat. It registered with him immediately that she was a good looking woman; not beautiful, or even pretty in the classic sense, but she was strikingly attractive. She was also very direct.

After introducing herself, she said, "You don't have a dog. Big place like this, plenty of room, you should have a dog." Everything about her approach, struck him wrong. If he had hackles, they'd be stiffly upright.

"I don't have a dog because I don't want a dog."

"What have you got against dogs? They're better than most humans."

"Nothing. I just don't want one; haven't got the time to take care of one."

"No wife, no kids, nothing but your work; you can make time. I think a dog is just what you need." She continued before he could object. "You've been here six months and you're like a bear with a sore head most of the time. Everybody in town knows it. You're the only one doesn't make conversation when he shops and that's okay. I don't think anyone wants to talk to you anyway. You live out here alone, surprise, surprise, and I think a dog would be the cure for whatever ails you.

"What do you say? I've got just the thing for you in my truck. Should I go get her?" She stood looking at him, hands on her hips and a challenge in her eyes.

He was tempted to tell her to get lost but there was something in what she said and the way she said it that hit him like a bucket of cold water. He heard himself asking, "What kind of dog?"

She smiled and he noticed it softened her expression and added to her attractiveness. "You're gonna love her. Sasha is a Czech Wolfdog."

"A *what*?"

"Relax, she's only part wolf. It's a new breed. They been working on this breeding program for a while and they've developed a dog that has the temperament, the pack mentality, and the trainability of the German Shepherd combined with the strength, physical build, and stamina of the Carpathian wolf. They're very versatile. They've been using them for search and rescue, tracking, herding, agility, obedience, and hunting. I don't normally approve of dog/wolf mixes, but this breed is something special."

"And what makes you think this dog is just the thing for me?"

She told him of the kind of environment the dog required, how the dog needed to be trained and worked, its personality and qualities. "I don't know what your story is, but I think this dog will bring you out of whatever place you're in right now. Do it right, and this dog will bond with you and make a better companion than 99% of the people you know. She needs someone special; so do you."

"And where did you get this canine marvel?"

"Rich guy imported her. Thought he was going to live here until his wife divorced him and took him to the cleaners. He had to leave. He can't have dogs where he is now. So? What do you say?"

"Let's see the dog."

One look and that was it. Stallings told him later she'd never seen a dog take to anyone the way Sasha took to him. It was immediate, as if the dog found the place she was meant to be and the person she was meant to be with. There was no way he could refuse. He acquired a dog and a friend.

On his fourth day back from Portland and his encounter with Marcie, Pat Stallings pulled up in front of the workshop. The structure was a converted barn. He'd turned the back third into a one bedroom apartment complete with kitchen, bathroom/shower, and spacious living room. After heavily insulating it and installing solar panels, it was a cosy retreat and more than adequate for his simple needs. The rest of the barn was devoted to a large workshop and storage area. Bins and racks lined one side while the rest housed a large workbench and assorted power tools, including a drill press and table saw.

The vet stepped out of her truck and Sasha bounded over to her. She just had time to wave before the big dog reached her and stood up to put its paws on her shoulders, tail wagging furiously. The woman rubbed the dog vigorously and then pushed her away.

"Hello Sasha, it's nice to see you too. How've you been, old girl?" She continued to rub the dog and scratch its ears for a minute, then straightened up and walked over to Dutch. "Just passing by and thought I'd stop in to see Sasha. And you too," she added as an after-thought.

"Nice to be included. How you keeping, doc?" He was starting to come out of the miserable state he'd worked himself into.

After he acquired Sasha, he saw quite a bit of the vet. He hadn't owned a dog since he was a kid, and never a breed as exotic as this one. He consulted with her frequently about care and training and she stopped by often to check on his progress. A casual friendship gradually developed. Because of the mood he was in, Dutch had spoken to her only briefly when he returned from Portland and picked up Sasha. The vet watched the dog for him on the odd occasions when he would be gone overnight or longer and could not take the animal with him.

"I'm fine. How's everything at Chez Yancy?"

He shrugged. "You know."

"How was the show? You didn't say much about it when you picked Her Nibs up. In fact, you didn't say much at all."

"It was late. Show was fine."

She frowned. He was being uncharacteristically reticent, even for him. "Sounds exciting. Laugh a minute was it?"

"Coffee?"

"Sure." She followed him into the kitchen and sat while he poured them both a cup. "Want to talk about it?"

"About what?"

"About whatever happened at the show."

"Why do you think something happened?"

She sighed. "Haven't you learned? You got back and you haven't been into town yet. You haven't ordered supplies, you haven't talked to anyone. People notice; people talk. You don't have to tell me anything, but if you want to talk about it, I'm listening."

He looked at his coffee cup for a while. "Had a visitor at the show; someone I used to know."

"A woman." It was a statement, not a question. In answer to his raised eyebrows and quizzical expression she said, "Usually what puts a man into isolation. You have all the symptoms."

He shrugged.

"What is she, ex-wife or just ex?"

He gave her a rueful smile. "Neither. I was travelling the wrong way on a one way street."

"Never much fun. She the reason you ended up here?"

"What makes you say that?"

"Lucky guess. So how was it?"

"I don't know; weird."

"Like 'I saw you last night and got that old feeling' weird?"

"No, not exactly. Actually, I just wanted her to go away. Seeing her dredged up a lot of stuff it took me a long time to get rid. I thought I put it all behind me. She shows up and I'm going through crap all over again."

She took a drink and looked at him over the rim of her cup. "Anything still there?"

He shook his head. "Nah. I'm just mad at myself for getting caught up in the memories. Maybe it wasn't a bad thing. I think I might have put her behind me, once and for all."

"That a good thing?"

"Oh, yes." For some reason, his answer made her happy.

He watched her stroke Sasha as she finished her coffee. She was a very good looking woman. She had a natural beauty that didn't require cosmetic enhancement. He thought makeup might actually detract from her looks. She didn't have a partner and, as far as he knew, she'd never been romantically linked with anyone. He wondered why. He didn't think she was a lesbian. On the few occasions he'd seem her outside of her professional capacity, she seemed equally at ease with either sex.

*Why haven't I asked her out? Why haven't I asked **anybody** out? Can't be because of Marcie . . . can it? Maybe I've just lost interest; early male menopause or something.*

Pat enjoyed Dutch. He was a good looking guy, with a sort of a refined ruggedness about him. He was easy going, never pushed, never pried, but didn't open up much either, although he was somewhat open with her. He didn't seem wary around her, unlike herself. She never noticed any animosity toward women from him. He just seemed, . . . disinterested.

He never made her feel uncomfortable with anything he said or did, not even in the way he looked at her. She was sure, from the look of frank appreciation he gave her more than once, that he found her attractive, but he never did or said anything to indicate he was interested in more than the casual friendship they shared. She wondered what she would do if a man asked her out.

"Since you facilitated such a wonderful therapy session this morning, and at such a reasonable price, how dinner Saturday?" It caught her completely off guard and she hesitated. "Come on Pat, don't give me the old, 'I never date patients'. ***Sasha*** is your patient, so that doesn't apply. You never date ***anybody***, far as I can tell, so this won't really be a date. Call it dinner with a friend. We can go to Portland, if you're worried about what people will say."

"*I* never date anyone? You're a fine one to talk."

He waggled his finger at her. "Procrastinating, doc. You trying to figure out how to turn me down politely? Much easier to accept, you know. What time should I pick you up?" *Why am I giving her the full court press? Gonna scare her off, sure as hell. Probably have to get a new vet.*

"Seven o'clock, and I don't like fish."

He smiled, relieved. "Right. Seven and no fish." *Well, no new vet — unless I screw this up. She's not smiling. Why isn't she smiling?*

"It's not terminal, it's only dinner. I promise, no proposal or anything."

She arched her eyebrows. "How disappointing." She looked at her watch. "Damn, I better go. Liz Holloway's shepherd is limping again." She got up and started for the door. He kept pace with her, Sasha trailing in the rear.

He walked her to her truck and opened the door. She got in and he closed the door behind her. She started the engine, then turned and looked at him. "Thanks, but don't make a habit of chivalrous gestures. Don't want people talking and ruining your reputation." She smiled, put the truck in reverse and turned around. He watched her drive away. He felt like a high school senior who'd just scored a prom date with the captain of the cheer squad.

Pat drove away surprised. She wasn't sure she'd done the right thing, but she felt surprisingly good having done it. She'd known Dutch Yancy almost as long as he'd been in Sholalla. Other than as a friend, she hadn't thought about him any more than any other man in town, single or married. She came here to practice veterinary medicine, not to get tangled up with a man. She'd had quite enough of that. He was easy going, maybe the easiest going man she'd ever met. He'd never shown the slightest interest in her, socially or romantically so his invitation took her totally by surprise. *Neatly done, Mr. Yancy.*

Chapter 5

"Willards, in Oregon City? Are you sure about this? They know you in Oregon City, and if they don't know you, they definitely know me. Are you sure that's where you want to go?"

"Yes, that's where I want to go. Worried?"

"No, of course I'm not worried - about myself. It's only 16 miles up to Oregon City and you can bet word'll spread in no time. You sure you're okay with that?"

"Listen Yancy, I appreciate you worrying about me and my reputation, but we haven't had any juicy gossip around here in a while. This will give folks something to talk about."

"Okay," grinned Dutch. "You do realize this won't do a thing for your reputation, but it'll do wonders for mine, don't you? People may stop thinking I'm gay"

"Maybe, maybe not," replied Pat. "It all depends on what I say when they ask me about it."

Dutch surprised her when he picked her up in his car, a lovingly restored '67 Ford Mustang convertible. She didn't know he owned anything but his van. His sport coat, shirt and tie she took as a compliment, telling her he considered this, and her, important.

He was equally impressed when she answered the door. He red hair fell in soft waves, instead of being bound up in the pony tail she usually affected. She wore makeup, but sparingly and very effectively. Her high heels brought her to within two inches of his height and enhanced a pair of legs any woman would envy and any man would love. She had on a jersey dress of emerald green that caressed every bit of her figure. She wasn't voluptuous, not an Ursula Andress, but her figure curved in and out in all the right places and in wonderful proportion.

"Wow," was the only word that came to mind, and it slipped out.

"Should I assume approval?"

"Sorry. I'm usually more descriptive, but you took me by surprise. I'm used to khaki, blue jeans, and boots."

"They're a lot more comfortable."

"At the risk of overstating, you look stunning."

"Thank you."

Everything about the meal was comfortable and enjoyable, for both of them. She ate like she enjoyed eating. He was interesting and interested. She listened and paid attention. She knew how to draw him out and when to back off. Her observations were perceptive, yet she knew how to keep the conversation in a light vein. Most of all, he appreciated her sense of humor. He could tease, knowing she'd give as good as she got.

Over coffee he said, "It's awfully hard for us to be inconspicuous when you look like you do."

"Did you want inconspicuous? You should have said. I could have changed and we could have gone to a hamburger joint." She didn't want him to know how much his compliment pleased her.

"Are you kidding? The minute we walked in here, every guy in the place wondered how I managed to score a date like you."

"This isn't date, remember?"

"Oh right, sorry; a dinner companion like you."

"Better. I'm pleased I could help."

"I'm pleased you're here."

She knew he was sincere and she stifled the quip that came to mind. She was glad also. "So am I."

He leaned forward and asked in a stage whisper, "What should we tell the home folks when they ask how it went?"

She leaned forward and responded in kind, "Just smile knowingly and raise your eyebrows. It'll drive them nuts."

He leaned back and smiled. "Very wicked. You know everyone will make up their own story."

"They will anyway. If you say nothing, there's always that element of doubt. You need to learn how to play the small town game."

"Seriously Pat, I don't want to do or say anything that will hurt your reputation. It's not important for guys, but it's different for a woman. I don't really know how it works in small towns, so you call the shots."

She smiled. "Thank you; that's sweet, but it really doesn't matter. People will call me for their animals, even if I have a scarlet letter hanging around my neck. Besides, if they talk about me they won't be talking about someone else."

"Very generous of you, but I think I'd be upset if I heard someone saying anything bad about you."

"Oh God, don't you dare! That's the *worst* thing you can do. That will only confirm their suspicions."

"But if I let it pass, won't that do the same thing?"

"Not if you smile enigmatically." She smiled, showing him an example. "See?"

He chuckled. "You never cease to amaze me."

"You thought I was only about animals?"

It was a mild evening so he put the top down on the way home. She moved the seat back and stretched out, laying her head back and watching the stars as he drove at a modest speed. It wasn't that he was being careful so the wind wouldn't rearrange her hair; he wanted to prolong the evening.

At her door, they faced each other. "Thanks, Dutch, I had a lovely time."

"Me too. Thanks for this evening."

She continued to look at him. "Is something wrong? All of a sudden you look, . . . I don't know . . ."

He smiled and looked down. "All of a sudden I feel very awkward. I want to kiss you but I don't want to ruin a wonderful evening." Her candor engendered a frankness in him.

"If you want to kiss me, why don't you?" She said it without thinking and without hesitation.

He hadn't kissed a woman in a very long time and holding her close, her warm soft lips against his, it was worth the wait. He could have stood there until morning, but there's an appropriate length of time for a kiss and he was sure he exceeded it. When they finally separated, he didn't want to let her go. He had to clear his throat ***and*** his head to manage the simple, "Thanks again, Pat."

She gently pushed herself back and said softly, "I had a nice time. Thank you." She turned and unlocked the door. Her voice was husky as she said, "Good night, Dutch."

"Good night, Pat."

He started down the steps as she slowly closed the door behind her. He sat in the car looking at the house for a minute before starting the engine. He was thinking about much more than kissing her on that porch. *Good thing common sense got the best of hormones – I think. That is a lot of woman, son. Why haven't I done this before? That was, . . . was, ...* he didn't even know *what* the right word was. When he pulled into his driveway, he wasn't sure how he'd gotten there.

Pat leaned her back against the door and listened for the sound of his engine. Some small part of her was hoping to hear a knock on the door. She stayed, even after she heard the engine start and the Mustang pull away. She pushed away from the door and walked slowly across the darkened room to the sofa. She wanted to think about the evening but that kiss kept getting in the way. It was disturbing. Pressed up against him, thoughts about more than kissing suddenly popped up and this was even ***more*** disturbing. Something told her to keep her distance from Dutch Yancy, at least for a while. Something equally strong was telling her she'd be a fool not to see him again, as soon as possible. *And here's **another** fine mess I've gotten me into!*

On opposites sides of Sholalla, Oregon, two people had trouble falling asleep, and for much the same reason. He was wondering *when* they could do it again. She was wondering if they *should* do it again. Both would like to repeat that kiss. Next morning, lying in bed thinking about the previous evening, Dutch and Pat had the identical thought. *I hope this doesn't screw up a perfectly good friendship!*

In New York, several hours earlier, Marcie Watson stared at the ceiling of her bedroom. *Why does love and romance and heat always have to screw up perfectly good working relationships?*

Dutch needed more wood for his burl clock creations. He went to town to pick up the chains for his chainsaw. He'd left them the previous week for sharpening. Sasha sat in the passenger seat, content to wait as she watched the passing foot traffic. Everyone in Sholalla knew Dutch and his wolfdog. They also knew enough to speak to Sasha as they passed, but not to approach the van. It wasn't that she would attack, but Sasha made it abundantly clear, she would not tolerate anyone tampering with the van, and passing too close was as good as tampering.

"Hi Bernie," Dutch called to the man behind the counter. "Got my chains?"

"Hey Dutch, how are you?"

"Better than nothing, so I've been told. Headed out to do some cutting. Need some more wood."

"Bring in some pictures when you get some more finished, will you? Nancy wants one to send her sister for Christmas. She wants to get all her shopping done early this year."

"Sure thing. How much do I owe you?"

"Let's see, three chains; that's $15.75."

Dutch paid and collected the sharpened chains. *These should hold me for three or four days cutting.* He crossed the street and was about to get into his van when he spotted Pat Stallings coming out of the drugstore. She was crossing the street to her truck parked a few spaces up the street from him. He hesitated, then put the chains in the van, scratched Sasha's ears, and walked toward Pat's truck.

"Hi," he said.

"Hi."

"How are you?"

"Fine. How are you?" she echoed.

Dutch had a tentative smile on his face, but he didn't feel like smiling. *This is weird. Why is this so weird? Why **should** it be weird? God damn it, we're both grownups. I'm not 16 and trying to keep my mother from finding out; then why do I **feel** like I'm 16?*

"Okay." *What to say now?* "You out on your rounds?"

"No, I just needed a few things for the office. What are you up to?"

"Just picking up some chains for the saw. I'm headed up toward Molina, looking for wood. I'm all out."

"Firewood?"

"Clocks."

"Oh."

He gave himself a mental slap. *Stop this crap!!*

"Can I ask you something?" She nodded. "Is it just me, or does this seem weird or awkward or something?"

She gave him a genuine smile. "I know. Why is that, anyway? I feel like a teenager who snuck out on a date with a biker and I'm waiting for my mother to find out."

He felt relieved to hear she was having the same difficulty. "Bernie didn't say anything, and you know what an old lady **he** is. I guess word hasn't got around yet." He looked directly into her eyes. "Truth is, Pat, I don't give a damn if it does. I had a great time and I would like to do it again. What about you?"

She hesitated. "I'm, . . . not sure, Dutch." *What are you afraid of? You **know** what you're afraid of!*

The disappointment made him feel like someone had just grabbed his stomach and squeezed. "Oh, I'm sorry. I thought, . . . well, I guess I thought you had as good a time as I did. My mistake." The deflation was evident in his tone. He took a deep breath. "Listen, it's okay, if you'd rather not; no harm, no foul. I better get on my way. Should have been there already. Late start this mornin'. I'll see you, doc."

He turned and walked back up the street, silently cursing himself for the idiot he was. *Just isn't worth it! Not a God damn one of 'em worth the tyin' yourself in knots over! I just never learn. You'd think by this time,. . . but hell no, not me.* He didn't hear her call out after him and he climbed into his van, made a U-turn, and drove away.

Pat Stallings looked after the van. He sounded disappointed but he acted angry. *I **don't** need an angry man in my life! I didn't say no. I was honest. Maybe I was too honest. I'm **not** sure. I could like him, probably way too much. I can't do this again. It hurts too much. Maybe he **is** different, but I can't take the chance. Why did I ever say yes in the first place?*

"Marcie? Are you all right?"

Startled, she looked up at the woman across the desk. "Yes, yes, of course."

"Are you sure? I've been here for five minutes," she exaggerated, "and I don't think you heard a word I said. Now who's going?"

"I'm sorry, Helene, going where?"

"Oh for pity sake! Seattle? Who's going to Seattle? Corbus, Trumpanion, remember?"

"Oh, yes, sorry. Who do we have that can make the trip?"

"Koku and Corman are both available."

"Not Koku, not to Seattle. Corman, maybe. Is he ready to do this?"

"I'm not sure. He could handle one. Two companies might be more than he's up to."

"So there's no one who can do both."

"Corman might, but he'd need someone along to support him. He's ready, he just doesn't think he is. If someone went along to hold his hand, it might be just what he needs to boost his confidence."

"Any handholders available?"

"Not really."

"We can't let this go. What about . . ." Marcie was looking at her and Hellene held up both hands in refusal.

"Absolutely not! I have waited two years for this holiday. We have the tickets booked, reservations in the Seychelles, and I am **not** putting my marriage on the line for a trip to Seattle; no way. Count me out!!"

"So that leaves me. I just came back from Portland, and now I have to turn around and fly back to Seattle, just to hold Corman's hand?"

"Life's tough at the top, boss."

Chapter 6

Dutch stayed angry all the way to Molina. He was angry because of the way Pat lead him on the night before, especially with their goodnight kiss, and then shot him out of the saddle this morning. More than that, he was angry with himself. *This is **not** going to be Marcie Watson all over again. That really would be some kind of insanity.*

As he approached Molina, he realized he was driving in excess of the limit and he slowed as he passed through the town to the woodland beyond. He concentrated on finding a place to park near the patch of woods he wanted to check. He was surprised to see a new Jeep Cherokee parked nearby. It was unusual to find hikers out here. It was the tail end of bear hunting season and cougar hunting season was year round, but there had been no reports of either animal in this locale, so he dismissed the idea of it being hunters.

He checked and prepped his small 10 inch chainsaw while Sasha waited patiently nearby. With a large empty knapsack on his back and his .357 revolver on his hip, he headed off into the woods. Sasha patrolled ahead and to either side. After an hour, he located a fallen white oak lying next to a large clump of shrubs. It had two large burls protruding from the trunk, one on the top, one on the side. He knelt for a closer look while Sasha rustled around in the shrubs, sniffing and pawing at the roots.

Suddenly there was a ripping and whining sound inches from his head, followed instantly by the sound of a gunshot. Only the fact that he was bent over examining the burls saved Dutch from the bullet. He threw himself behind the fallen log and quietly called Sasha to him. Without conscious thought he found his .357 revolver in his hand. He did not venture into the woods without it.

There was a rustling in the shrubs as Sasha emerged and leaped over the log to land beside him, just ahead of another shot. He placed a restraining hand on her neck as she lay beside him. He whispered to her to be silent while he waited, ears straining.

After a few moments he heard the sound of someone moving through the brush and a voice called out, "Over here. I'm pretty sure I got him." Dutch waited until the footsteps got closer, then cautiously raised his head to peer over the log.

Through the gaps in the brush he could see two people approaching the brush in front of him. He let them get to within 10 yards, then he stood and pointed his pistol at two men. "Stop right there! Drop your weapons and raise your hands." The men stopped, surprised and confused. Dutch shouted, "Drop your weapons! I won't tell you again."

The first man complied, then the second man, somewhat more slowly. Dutch eased himself over the log and around the brush to approach the pair. The second man had moved up and was standing next to the first, both with their hands raised. They were looking at each other with confused expressions which slowly changed as the realized what they had done.

"Why you were shooting at me?" asked Dutch.

"We didn't mean to shoot at you mister, honest" said the first man. "We didn't know you were there."

"Then why did you?"

"Like I said, we didn't know you were there. When we saw and heard the brush move we figured it was a bear or maybe a cougar. We have permits for both."

"Do I *look* like a goddamn bear or cougar?"

"Nuh, nuh, no," came the stuttered response. So far only the first man had spoken.

"Did you actually *see* a bear or cougar?"

"Well, . . ah, . . . no."

"Then what the hell were you shooting at?"

"When the bush, . . .that is, I ah, . . . I thought when I saw, . . ."

"You stupid shit for brains; the bush moved and you shot, that's what happened isn't it? You didn't see a goddamned thing! The bush moved and you took a chance and were trying to kill whatever was there."

"Well, uh, . . . when you put it that way, uh . . . I guess so."

"You coulda killed me! You realize that? Do you? Worse than that, you coulda killed my dog. Suppose I return the favor; I'll give you a hundred yards head start, then I'll send Sasha after you. How about that?"

Sasha was standing beside him, head down, slightly stooped, fangs bared in response to the sound of her master's rising anger. Both hunters took a step back when they looked at her. "Hey, come on mister. You wouldn't do that, would you?" This was the first time the second man said anything.

Dutch silently regarded the pair, a look of sheer disgust on his face. "Back up! Go on, back up!" He motioned with his weapon. The pair complied. Dutch moved forward and Sasha moved with him. Both the men now kept their eyes riveted on the dog.

He picked up both rifles, noting that they were expensive looking, probably custom made, and worth upwards of $1,000. Dutch said to Sasha, "Guard them, Sasha. If they run, rip their throats out." The dog didn't understand anything other than she was to watch the two men, but they didn't know that.

He walked over to the fallen tree and swung each rifle against the tree as hard as he could, breaking the stock apart. Then he pulled out the bolt from each and threw it as far away as possible. When he finished, he returned to the dog. Neither man had moved a step, nor had they taken their eyes from Sasha.

"Now you two get the hell out of my woods. You ever take a bush shot again and I hear about it, Sasha and I will be paying you a visit and you will not enjoy it. Now git!" He motioned with his weapon and the pair turned and hurried away without a word of protest. Sasha followed for several steps until Dutch called her back.

"That's okay, Sasha, let 'em go. Come on, girl. I got work to do."

It was the next day when Corby Danvers pulled up in front of his shop. Dutch was inside examining the burls he'd taken from the fallen white oak as well as some red alder burls and didn't hear him arrive.

"Hey Dutch," called Danvers as he entered.

Dutch looked up. "Hey Chief, how are you? What brings you out this way?"

Danvers sauntered over to the workbench. "See ya got some burls. New stuff?"

"Yeah; just cut it yesterday."

"Up near Molina?"

Dutch turned to face the policeman. "Matter of fact. Why?"

"Anything happen while you were over there? You have a run in with anybody?"

"What's this about, Corby?"

"Appreciate an answer, Dutch; you have a run in with anyone back in the woods?"

"So happens I did. Why? What's the problem?"

"Couple of hunters filed a complaint with the Molina Police. Said a man with a dog that looked like a wolf held them up and stole their rifles. You know anything about that?"

"Come on back and have a coffee."

"Rather have an answer, Dutch."

"Come on back; you can have an answer *and* a coffee."

Forty-five minutes later Danvers was finishing his second cup. "Shouldn't be any trouble over this. They may be a couple of high priced lawyers from Portland, but faced with attempted murder, or attempted manslaughter, or reckless endangerment charges, I'm pretty sure they'll drop the complaint. Too bad they can't find a way to keep yahoos like that out of the woods."

"Maybe they'll know better in future – but I doubt it."

"Not 'til they shoot someone. Let's hope somebody gets them first." Danvers stood to go. "Bush shooters – I hate those assholes. Every year seems like I'm pickin' up a body or takin' a statement in the hospital from someone shot by one of those damn bush shooters." He shook his head. "Too bad you didn't use their heads to break up their rifles instead of an innocent tree trunk. Well, thanks for the coffee, Dutch. Oh yeah, congratulations. 'Bout time someone took Pat Stallings out. Beginning to worry about her. How'd that go, by the way?"

Dutch hesitated before he replied, "Fine, but don't read too much into it. We're just friends."

Something in his tone caused Danvers to look closely at the clock maker. "Things gotta start someplace. Thanks for the coffee, Dutch. Best be on my way." He reached down and rubbed his hand across Sasha's head. "So long, girl."

It was three days since he'd seen Pat in town. He had a nice collection of white oak and red alder burls but try as he might, he simply couldn't get started on slicing and working the wood. When he looked at a burl, at it's pattern, at the swirls and waves, he could see what he needed to do and visualize what it would look like when he finished. The wood had a way of speaking to him, but its voice was silent now.

He was still upset by the encounter with Pat in town, overlaid with his feelings about the chance meeting with Marcie Watson. More than anything, he was angry with himself. Three years and Marcie could still upset him. He was over her. He *was* over her. All that teenage, unrequited love angst crap, that was over. So why did it upset him?

*And Pat Stallings; what about Pat? So, it was a little weird in town. If the date worked for me but it didn't work for her, those things happen; they happen all the time. But, (why the hell was there **always** a but) what about that kiss?* He was sure she felt something. *He* damned sure felt something! Why did she put him off like that?

Here he was, couldn't work, out of sorts, didn't want to talk to anybody. Even Sasha was fed up with him. He was fed up with himself. Something had to change. Best thing to do was leave everything and get away for a couple of days. A total change of scene, that was what he needed – what they both needed.

He called Leroy Nelson in Lake Oswego and arranged to come for a short visit. He threw a few things in a bag, gathered up Sasha's bed, food and dishes, and drove to the Portland suburb.

About an hour after Dutch left, Pat Stallings pulled into his drive. She'd been distracted and upset ever since Dutch had stalked off. She blamed herself and she had wrestled with the problem of what to say with him. She wasn't completely sure she knew exactly what to say even now, but she didn't want to let it go any longer. He deserved better. She had to talk to him – except he wasn't there.

She looked around, but his place was locked up tight and there was no sign of Sasha. For a fleeting moment she had the awful thought that he'd left for good, but realized that was only her own fears speaking. Through the windows she could see his equipment and tools. Surely he wouldn't go anywhere without those. There was no note stuck in the door. She called his number and got the voice mail message, but nothing about his being away. She wasn't sure what to think.

In her Seattle hotel room, Marcie Watson hung up the phone. That was the fifth time she called and the fifth time she'd left a message. She finished with the meetings yesterday, but delayed her departure. She really needed to talk to Dutch. After her final meeting, she'd called Arthur to let him know the result and that they were on their way back. The conversation got very interesting, very quickly.

"Dutch lives pretty close to Seattle, doesn't he?"

"Down near Portland someplace; a three or four hour drive I guess. Why?"

"One of our new clients was in this morning and saw that clock Dutch gave you hanging on the wall of your office. He really liked it; wanted to know where you got it."

"What's his interest?"

"He has the biggest line of high end decorative room accessories in the Northeast. He's starting a new line; Early American rustic, he calls it. He thinks clocks like that would fit in perfectly. Think Dutch might be interested?"

She was suddenly aware of myriad possibilities, all of them attractive. "I don't know, Arthur. Can you put me in contact with the client so I can get some idea of what he needs?"

An hour later she put down the phone and sat back, deep in thought. This was an amazing opportunity, not only for Dutch, but for her. If he was interested and he and the client could agree terms, there was a perfect path to bring the big Dutchman right back into her life. *And why wouldn't Dutch want this? My God, the initial order would be a six figure deal! What an opportunity. He could step right up into the major leagues – big time. And it would make sense for him to move back to New York. They have trees in New York, **and** Vermont, **and** New Hampshire. I have **got** to get hold of him!*

She thought about it and decided that she'd try for the rest of the day to contact him. If she had no luck, she would drive down to see him. She would have to do the sales job of her life but she'd had tougher challenges – hadn't she?

She called all day without success. Either he was there and he didn't want to speak to her or he was away. If he was away, where; for how long? Maybe this was going to be tougher than she originally thought. Her inability to contact him was raising doubts. This wasn't like her. She was many things, but she was ***never*** indecisive.

In addition, although she wasn't sure Arthur was right, there was still unfinished business between her and Dutch. She needed to resolve it and the sooner the better, especially if he was coming back to New York. *That's the ticket girl; think positive!* This Sholalla wasn't that far away; Oregon wasn't ***that*** big.

Dutch always felt better after a visit with Leroy and his family; better and a little envious. Leroy and LeeAnn, his wife, had been sweethearts since 10th grade. There was never any doubt in their minds that they would marry. They were sweethearts all through high school and Leroy's time in the Army. They married a few days after his discharge and now had two beautiful and lively children, Brian, age 5, and Melissa, who was 4. They lived in one of the largest houses on the lake, a gift from his father. It had been the Nelson family home, and when William Nelson retired and moved to France with his French wife, he'd given the house to his son. Leroy now ran the largest real estate business in Lake Oswego.

It was always a big event for the children when their 'Uncle' Dutch came for a visit. He was great fun but, more importantly, he always brought Sasha. There was an instant bond between the dog and the children, from the moment they met. His visits were a joyous occasion for all of them. While the adults talked, the two children and the animal rolled and tumbled and played chase across the lawn, into and out of the water. If the children got too rough, Sasha signalled with a growl. If they persisted, Sasha would retire to the house and lie down until the children coaxed her out again. She would return and the children would be gentler in their play.

The adults were seated on the patio, watching the trio on the lawn. On his second beer, Dutch had just finished explaining about Marcie's sudden appearance, his date with Pat Stallings, and their subsequent meeting in town next day.

"I don't know. What do you think?" he asked Leroy.

"You're asking the wrong cowboy. What I know about women you could write on a matchstick. It took me five years just to figure out how to buy Christmas and birthday presents for this one," he said, motioning toward his wife. "You should ask her."

Dutch looked at LeeAnn. The pretty petite blonde shrugged. "It's really hard to say without knowing either of them, Dutch. Did Marcie say anything about how she felt about you, either now or before?"

"She made some reference to people missing me, but I don't know what people or if she meant herself. That was all."

"Maybe it was just what it seemed, a surprise meeting between two people who used to work together. Did she ask for your number or address?"

"No," he admitted.

"Are you wondering how she feels, or are you worried about how you feel?"

"I don't know; some of each maybe."

"How **do** you feel?"

He'd been trying to figure that out. "Surprised, I guess. Of course I was surprised to see her out of the blue like that. I'm more surprised that it bothered me like it did."

"Bothered you in what way?"

He thought for a moment. "It dredged up a lot of feelings I thought were dead and buried. I thought I was done with her. I thought I put all that . . . her, behind me. I hadn't even thought about her in a while and then, there she was. I didn't really **want** to have breakfast with her, to tell the truth."

LeeAnn smiled. "It sounds like you don't have anything to worry about. I think the memories that came back threw you. You can't expect them to disappear completely. You worked with her for three years and she was the reason you moved all the way across the country. I expect she'll fade into the background more as time goes by."

"I hope you're right. Pat's the one that has me stumped. I can't figure out what's going on. We've been friends almost from the time I moved to Sholalla. She stops by all the time. We had a wonderful time at dinner. I didn't intend to kiss her, it just sort of happened."

"What was her reaction?"

"She liked it; at least I'm pretty sure she did. She didn't pull away or slap me afterwards. It seemed like it was something, if you know what I mean. But then, in town next morning, it was awkward, like she didn't know what to say to me. Truth is, I wasn't sure what to say to her either. When I told her I'd like to do it again, dinner I mean, she hesitated and I could feel her pull away. She said she wasn't sure; just blew me off."

"Did you ask her why?"

"No," he admitted.

LeeAnn leaned forward, intrigued. "What did you do?"

"I got mad," he admitted. "I told her I thought she had a good time too and it was okay if she didn't want to do it again."

"What did she say then?"

"I don't know."

"Why not?"

"I walked away."

"Oh." LeeAnn sat back in her chair and sipped her lemonade. He kept waiting for her to say something, but she was silent. Leroy was getting uncomfortable.

Finally Dutch asked, "Well, what do you think?"

"You don't want to know what I think."

He was surprised. "That bad? All right, come on, tell me."

"You asked for it. Dutch, you didn't walk away, you ran. Honestly, you men will face gunfire, flood, fire, typhoon, and hurricane, but you bolt as soon as there's an emotional problem. No wonder women have to do everything in relationships. If we didn't, there wouldn't be any!"

"Go ahead, LeeAnn, don't sugar coat it; tell me what you really think."

She grinned. "I'm sorry, Dutch, but honestly, why *didn't* you talk to her about it? Obviously there's something bothering her. If she enjoyed the kiss as much as you did and then reacted that way later, it sounds like a case of second thoughts or second guessing or second something. You need to find out what's going on, what it is that's bothering her, instead of guessing or deciding you know how she feels. You *don't* know how she feels, any more than I do. Don't talk to me, talk to her."

He smiled ruefully. "You're right, as usual. It was childish to get mad and walk away like that. She was the first woman I've taken out since I've been here and I guess I was hoping for more, especially after . . . . ." He sighed. "I'll see her when I get back. Maybe she just doesn't want to get involved, at least not with me. I'll have to find out."

Before he left he told Leroy, "You're a lucky man Nelson, I envy you. You've got LeeAnn and the kids, great house, successful business. You have everything in life any man could ask for. I hope I'm as lucky as you are someday."

"Ain't luck, pal; we work at it."

He was in a lighter mood on his way back to Sholalla. He always felt good after a visit with the Nelsons. Sasha was asleep on the seat beside him. She was exhausted after two days of near constant activity with the children.

He made a quick stop at home and dropped off his bag. There were several messages on his answer phone but he decided to check them when he got back. He needed to go to the bank first. When he got back into the truck, he realized his rifle was still under the seat and his pistol was in the glove box. They had been there ever since his trip to Molina. Rather than leave them at home, he decided keep them with him for now. Once he got back home, he could relax and call Pat.

Pat Stallings was just leaving her house. She needed to stop by the bank and deposit several checks.

Marcie Watson had given up and was returning to Sholalla. She'd left Seattle early that morning and made good time. She found Sholalla without any trouble, but she couldn't find the road where ***It's About Time*** was located. She decided to stop at the only bank in town. They must know Dutch and could give her directions to his place.

Other people had also decided to visit the Columbus Bank branch on Grange Street that day. Four men in a stolen Ford Explorer were on the way into Sholalla. A police car passed them headed out of town in response to reports of a non-existent accident on Highway 211 east of town. They waited patiently for a parking place directly in front of the bank. Once parked, they waited until the number of customers inside thinned out.

At 11:05 Pat Stallings walked into the bank to make her deposit.

At 11:07 Marcie Watson walked into the bank to inquire how to get to Dutch Yancy's workshop.

At 11:09 Dutch Yancy pulled up and parked a block and a half away from the bank. He walked slowly up the sidewalk. A half a block from the bank he ran into Rusty Jacobs from Samson's Hardware.

"Say Dutch, someone said you took Doc Stallings out to dinner the other night over in Oregon City. That right?"

"Now where'd you hear that?"

"I don't know, somebody said you had. That true? How was it? I didn't know the doc went out with anybody. Nice lady, Pat is."

He was saved from coming up with a 'I can neither confirm or deny' answer when there came the unmistakable sound of shoth from the direction of the bank. The two men looked at each other.

"Say, Dutch, that sounded like, . . ."

"Yeah, it was. Those shots came from the bank."

Neither moved for a moment, then Dutch moved toward the store front beside them, pushing Rusty ahead of him. "Let's get the hell out of the line of fire."

Shortly afterwards, he saw three men exit the bank. One of them had what looked like an assault rifle and a large sack. The other two carried hand guns and each was dragging a woman. One of the men saw Dutch and Rusty and threw a hasty shot in their direction before disappearing around the corner.

"You okay?"

"Yeah Dutch. What the hell's going on?"

"Looks like three guys just robbed the bank and were dragging couple of women with them; probably hostages. You check the bank. I'll go ahead and follow them until the police can catch up."

He turned and sprinted for his van. When he got there, Sasha was sitting up, alarmed and anxious, alerted by the shots.

As he climbed in he said, "Easy girl, it's okay. We're going to take a little ride." He started the engine and pulled away from the curb, tires screeching. He didn't have any time to lose if he wanted to keep whatever the getaway vehicle was in sight.

He took the corner, tires screaming in protest, and caught a glimpse of a maroon SUV rapidly disappearing in the distance. He pushed his van to the limit. He hoped they were strangers. His only advantage would be his knowledge of the road. He did some calculations while he drove.

David Vaillancour

Estacada's 20 miles and then we hit 224. 224 will take them into Hood National Forest or they can stay on 211 up to Sandy and take State 26, east into Portland and Interstate 205, or west into the Hood. Better call 911 and tell them where I am and what I'm doing.

Chapter 7

Inside the maroon Maverick SUV, there was a great deal of shouting, swearing, and recrimination among the three gunmen. The only one keeping silent was the driver. As they sped down the main road out of town, the man in passenger seat turned and shouted at the two in back, "God damn it! What the fuck were you doing? You stupid son of a bitch! I told you no shooting!"

"The old bastard didn't give me any choice! Besides, you said there was no guard."

"He *wasn't* a guard, you fuckin' idiot! He was the greeter at the door, just like I told you."

"Well, he was dressed like a guard and he looked like he was reaching for his gun," said the man sullenly.

"Don't bullshit me, you fuck! His hands were in the air. God damn it! I told you nobody in the bank had a gun. That's what made it so easy. That's why I picked it. No guns! Do you understand mother fuckin' English, you fuckin' moron? Didn't I say there were no guns? What part of no guns don't you understand?" He turned and looked at the driver.

"Leave me outta this. I drive, I fly, I don't do guns. I don't do kidnapping, either."

"It looks like you do now." He turned back to the pair in the rear, this time talking to the other man. "And you, you jackass, I outta shoot your ass right now! I told you to leave them." He nodded at Pat, seated between them and Marcie, huddled on the floor. "Bank robbery is one thing, but nothin' gets the FBI on your ass quicker than kidnapping. Nothin'! Now we'll have local, state, *and* feds after our asses. Well done, stupid!"

"Relax, Mase, relax. Ain't nobody on our ass. The cops are all outta town and by the time the State Police or FBI gets here, we'll be long gone, *long* gone, thanks to Smilin' Jack here." He kicked the back of the driver's seat.

"Yeah Mase," chimed in the other man. "A little fluff along always makes the trip nicer. They might come in handy, if we get in a tight spot, and besides, we might have a little fun along the way." He reached over and squeezed Pat Stallings thigh.

She pushed his hand away. "Keep your hands off me, you pig." Marcie gave a small frightened whimper.

He broke into a leering, evil smile. "Sweetheart, I'll be grabbin' a lot more than your leg before I'm through."

"Ross, shut up!" barked the man in front. "You and that halfwit half brother of yours have caused enough trouble. Now shut up, and keep your goddamn hands to yourself!"

Before Dutch could dial 911, his phone rang. "Yancy."

"Dutch, this is Rusty. Where are you?"

"Behind them on 211, about 5 miles out of town. What's the story?"

"They robbed the bank and shot old Maurice twice. He's pretty bad. Paramedics are on the way."

"Who are the two women?"

"One of 'em's Pat Stallings, other one's a stranger. Listen Dutch, you be careful. These guys don't fool around. Maurice was standing there with his hands up when one of them shot him, just like that. No reason, just shot him."

"Rusty, tell the police where I am. I'll call when I can and keep them posted. Tell them to hurry. See if they can get the Estacada cops to put up a roadblock at 224, but they gotta hurry"

"Okay. Dutch, you armed?"

"What?"

"Have you got any guns?"

"No, I . . . wait a minute. Yeah. I've got my rifle and .357. I forgot to take them out when I was cutting last time."

"You be careful. Don't want anybody else to get hurt."

"Don't worry." He clicked off.

"The turnoff is just up here. Slow down, Flyboy," directed Mase. "There, right there. See it?"

The driver swung off the road and onto what was once a driveway.

Dutch rounded the curve and felt a moment of panic. He couldn't see the maroon Maverick. It was only about a half mile ahead of him and now it was gone, nowhere in sight on the two mile stretch of road ahead. *Where the hell did they go? They can't have gotten that far ahead of me **that** fast. They must have turned off, but there are no side roads for the next few miles. They couldn't have driven off the road; ditch is too steep. So where the hell are they?*

Then he remembered – the old Miller place. It was an abandon farm, with a dilapidated wreck of a house that hadn't been lived in for more than 20 years. He sometimes cut burls in the woods behind the farm. *Why would they turn off there? No place to go if you do; no way to cut through the woods. They wouldn't do it thinking it was a road or some way through the woods, especially if they aren't familiar with the area; too risky. So why, . . . unless they're changing cars. Has to be it. Where is that drive? It's here someplace.*

He slowed down and then he saw it, the faint track leading off the road, over a culvert, and down a lane lined with thick brush and trees. He stopped on the shoulder and got out, fishing under the seat for the rifle he stored there a few days before. He checked the glove box and found his .357 revolver, half a box of rifle cartridges, and a full box of shells for the handgun. Sasha was standing on the seat, alert, anxious.

"Easy girl, it's okay." He ran his hand across her head. Putting the cartridges in the cargo pockets of his pants, he got back in the van and pulled it forward, across the drive. *Well boys, unless you can figure a way to leap that ditch, you're screwed. No place to go from here.* The terrain behind the house was too rough and overgrown for anything short of a tank to negotiate. He got out and called Sasha. With his pocket knife, he quickly slashed all four tires, then locked the truck. *You won't be moving this in a hurry.*

Calling for Sasha to follow, he ran across the highway and hurried into the fringe of trees that bordered the road. He found a concealed spot that gave him a clear view of his van, and a clear field of fire. He put Sasha in a down, and settled in to wait.

"Come on, goddamn it, move!" Mase was in a hurry and no one was moving fast enough to suit him. Flyboy had parked behind the partially collapsed house next to a black Chevy Silverado. They all got out. One of the men in the back pulled Marcie from the vehicle and none too gently. As they started to get into the Silverado, Mase stopped them.

"She's in front with me." He pointed at Marcie. "Del, you and your brother sit in back with her." He motioned toward Pat. Before they moved, he added, "No fuckin' around back there. After we get to the chopper, you do what you want, but not until. You got me?" He stared at Del.

"Yeah, sure Mase, I got you – for now."

Mase turned to face him fully. "You got something you wanna say to me, Del?"

The other man smiled. "Nah Mase, not now."

"Anytime, Del. You just let me know. How 'bout you, Abe? Anything you wanna say?" he said to the other brother.

"Me? Hell no. Whatcha mad at me fer? I didn't do nothin'"

"The hell you didn't. I told you to leave these two." He nodded toward the women.

"Yeah, but Del, he said . . . ."

"I don't give a fuck what that half wit brother of yours said. He ain't runnin' this goddamn show – *I* am!" He looked at Del, but his challenge wasn't taken up. They climbed into the Silverado, pushing the women ahead of them. Flyboy drove back up the long drive toward the highway. As he eased past a large shrub that had grown across the drive, he saw Dutch's van blocking the entrance.

"What the fuck?" snarled Mase. Flyboy stopped 10 feet from the van.

Mase looked around carefully. Seeing nothing, he slowly opened the door and eased his way out. AK-47 at the ready, he stepped away from the Chevy, looking all around.

"Del, with me."

The back door opened and Del stepped out, equally cautious. He had traded his pistol for an H&K MP-5 submachine gun.

"Cover me," said Mase, and he walked slowly up to the van. He noted that the tires were flat as he tried the locked door. *What the fuck is going on here? Where did this come from? Who the hell is this guy and where is he?* He looked at the drainage ditch that ran alongside the road. *Can't drive through that. We gotta move this thing.*

Mase raised his weapon to smash the window. The ground near him exploded with flying gravel and dirt at the same instant he heard the flat crack of a shot. He ducked and froze. Behind him, Del sought cover behind the open door of the Chevy.

Both men crouched, waiting. The silence following the shot was eerie. Mase was trying to figure out where the shot came from. *He must be across the road somewhere.* He cautiously raised his head until he could see over the rim of the van's window. *In those trees. Lotta goddamn cover over there and not shit over here. He's got us cold.* He ducked back down, his mind racing.

"Mase. You see anything?"

"Nah. He's across the road in those trees I think."

"Who the hell is it?"

"Don' know. Ain't cops or they'd a said somethin'."

"So whadda we do?"

Mase didn't answer. *We can't stay here. We gotta go – now! We're falling behind schedule. They'll block the road soon and then we're fucked. It'll be all over. We gotta move this thing.* He looked behind him. *We'll push it outta the way.*

"Get back in the truck," he called to Del. Mase moved quickly back and got in. "Flyboy, ease up and push that thing outta the way."

"I ain't sure it's got the power, Mase."

"Just push against one end, front or rear. Pivot it around enough so we can get by."

Dutch watched as the Chevy started slowly forward. *What are they, . . . oh no you don't.*

He sighted carefully, then fired. The bullet struck the back tire, flattening it almost instantly and jarring the occupants. The Chevy stopped immediately. Dutch worked the bolt and chambered a fresh round. While he waited for their next move, he removed the magazine and refilled it with the loose rounds in his pocket.

Inside the Chevy, Mase was starting to worry. He desperately wanted to get out of this driveway and onto the highway, flat tire or not.

"Try it, Flyboy. Go on, push the damn thing outta the way."

"I dunno if I can get enough traction with one flat tire."

"Try anyway. We ain't got much time."

"Come on, Flyboy, get us outta here!" Abe spoke up, worried, on the verge of panic.

Flyboy eased the Chevy forward. There was a loud noise from another shot. The front tire exploded and there was a jar as the vehicle suddenly dropped slightly to the right.

"Back up!" shouted Mase. "Get us back behind the house!"

Dutch watched as the Chevy backed rapidly down the drive on two flat tires. The driver was having difficulty keeping it out of the shrubs, but managed to steer it out of sight back along the drive.

So what now, boys? You got the other SUV but you can't come this out way and you can't cross the ditch. The woods? He tried to remember what was east, beyond the farm. That was where he cut burls. *You might get a little way, but not far and not for long.*

He rose. "Sasha. Close."

He started out of the trees, cautiously. Keeping low, he ran to the drainage ditch, the dog beside him, alert to his every move. He hunkered down in the ditch and peered over the edge. He saw no movement. Then he heard the sound of an engine starting. It told him all he needed to know.

"Everybody in the car. Come on; let's go. Now!"

They all piled out of the crippled Chevy and into the SUV. "You," Mace directed Marcie, "sit on her lap." He pointed at Pat. "Flyboy, head for the woods." He motioned toward the trees across the field at the back of the old farmhouse.

"You sure about this, Mace?"

"Listen Flyboy, if we can't drive out, whoever the fuck it is sure as shit can't drive in after us. Drive as far east as you can, then we'll hike to the chopper. If he trails us, we'll take him in the woods." Flyboy put the Ford in gear and headed across the overgrown yard toward the field and the woods beyond.

Dutch moved toward the house, using the row of tall shrubs and bushes for cover. He moved quickly but cautiously, depending upon Sasha to warn him where someone might be lying in ambush. The dog moved with him, alert, but giving no warning.

Dumb shits. Could have dropped a trailer to pick me off as I came up: circle back and pick him up later. Dumb shits.

He got near the rear of the house and worked his way through the overgrown shrubs and bushes until he had a clear view of the back of the house and yard. There was only the disabled Chevy Silverado; no sign of anyone waiting in ambush. Sasha was not giving an alert signal. Stepping out of the brush, he looked toward the field. In the distance he could see the Ford Maverick just entering the woods. *They won't get far in that thing. Better check in with Rusty.*

The cell phone signal was weak but he was able to get through. "Hey Rusty, can you hear me?"

"Yeah Dutch, where are you?"

"Old Miller place, out toward Estacada. They're headed east, into the woods, toward the Hood. They're still in the Maverick."

"They can't get far in those woods, even in an SUV. What are they doing?"

"Didn't have time to ask 'em. They still got the hostages. Any idea who the other one was?"

"You might know her."

"*I* might know her? Why's that?"

"She was askin' directions to your place."

"My place? What'd she look like?"

"Dunno. Marlene said she was dressed pretty stylish and she talked like she was from back east someplace, maybe New York."

"Shit!" *Marcie. Has to be. What the hell's she doing here? Shoulda checked my messages. Goddamn woman is still complicating my life.*

"Okay, Rusty. Sasha and I are going in after them. Tell the cops to take it easy. We don't need to get taken out by friendly fire. I don't think the phone signal will be very good back in those woods. If it is, I'll keep them posted. Gotta go."

"Good luck, Dutch. You be careful. Remember, those guys shot Marvin when he had his hands up."

"No need to remind me. Don't worry, I'll be fine. I just want to stop them getting away with the hostages." He stuck the phone in his pocket.

Chapter 8

The going wasn't bad for the first half mile or so. The trees were thinly spread and there weren't many fallen ones to avoid. The undergrowth was mostly fern and the ground fairly level. Flyboy kept the Ford in four wheel drive as he manoeuvred between the tall pines.

"How far you figure it is to the chopper?" asked Mase.

"Eight, maybe ten miles."

"How long to get there?"

"Long time."

"Why? We're making pretty good time right now."

"Right now."

"What the hell does that mean?" Mase's temper was getting shorter by the minute.

"Because the stuff we're in now won't last long. The deeper in we get, the worse it will be. So far the brush is pretty thin *and* the trees aren't thick *and* there aren't too many downed trees *and* there aren't any rivers or creeks to cross. The brush will get heavy *and* the trees will get a lot thicker *and* there'll be a lot of downed trees *and* we'll hit some kind of creek or small river with a steep bank we can't negotiate. That's when we stop riding and start walking."

"Well aren't you a cheery bastard? How do you know all this?"

"It's Oregon. That's the kind of woods they have in Oregon."

"Jesus, you must have been raised on some kind of sour milk. You're the most pessimistic bastard I ever saw."

"Realistic, that's all."

Just 200 yards later, Flyboy was proven right. He was stopped by a large fallen tree. He reversed and tried to find a way around but, no matter which way he went, thick brush, fallen trees, or a steep creek bank blocked his path.

"No use, Mase. We have two choices; we can backtrack and look for another way, or start walking."

Mase was angry and frustrated. Nothing was going according to plan. *This bank was only the **test** run. An easy test run. God damn it! That fuckin' asshole. Who the fuck is he anyway? What's he doin', playin' John Wayne? This ain't some goddamned western. Son of a bitch!* "Come on, we walk."

"Aw Jesus, Mase," whined Del. "We ain't dressed for no hike in the wilderness."

"We don't have a choice, stupid. You got a better idea? I don't know how far behind us the cops are. The guy that shot at us probably already told them where the farm is. They'll have as tough a time in this stuff as we will. They won't be any better equipped than we are. Now get out; we walk to the chopper."

"What **about** that asshole who shot at us?"

"What about him?"

"You figure he's alone?"

"Probably. There was only one guy shootin' at us."

"You figure he's followin' us?"

"Four of us, one of him? Not if he's smart, he ain't. Even if he is, he's got no wheels, so we got a big head start."

"Yeah, but, . . ."

"But nothin. Listen; when you're trailin' somebody and they're armed, even if you ain't outnumbered, ya gotta be careful. Ya gotta take it slow, in case they try to ambush you."

"We gonna do that?"

"Why? You wanna stay behind and wait to see if he's followin' us, you be my guest." Del's face expressed his answer. "Yeah, me neither. We only do that if we ***know*** he's behind us and getting' close Now come on; we can't waste any more time. Grab everything and let's go."

They piled out and took knapsacks from the rear luggage area. Del and Abe donned one each and Mase put the money from the robbery in a third, which he put on.

Del watched him closely. "How come *you're* carryin' the money, Mase?"

"Because I'm the only one I trust. You keep an eye on these two." He indicated the women. "We gotta move fast as we can. Make sure they keep up."

Dutch arrived at the back of the farmhouse just in time to see the Ford Maverick disappear into the trees. He checked the Chevy for keys – missing. He didn't think they would set up an ambush. They were in a hurry and they probably didn't think he'd follow them anyway; at least that's what he hoped.

There was never been a question about whether he should go after them. As long as Pat and Marcie were with them and no police in sight, it was up to him. Keeping Sasha close, Dutch worried the entire way across the field. It was covered in tall weeds and shrubs. Adequate cover, but not while he was moving as fast as he was.

He made good time with Sasha keeping pace beside him. At the edge of the woods he stopped to listen. He couldn't hear the Ford. They must be quite a way ahead; either that or the woods absorbed the sound of the engine. He checked his cell phone – no signal. No surprise.

He could plainly see the tracks of the SUV. He followed them, keeping as far to one side of the tracks as he could while still keeping them in sight. *No sense giving them any better target than I have to.*

He stopped every 50 yards or so to listen and to give Sasha a chance to sniff the air. He wished he had some water; they'd be thirsty later. They would probably cross some small creeks and they could drink then. He was more worried about Sasha than himself. He was wearing regular boots, not his hiking boots. *Not the best thing in this terrain, but those guys won't be any better off.*

The going was easy and he made good time. They had covered about 1000 yards when Sasha gave a low growl. He stopped and knelt beside the big grey dog. She was looking intently ahead and slightly to the right. He checked his rifle to ensure there was a round in the chamber. Man and dog moved forward cautiously, until he spotted the Maverick. He circled around, keeping 50 feet between himself and the vehicle. Satisfied it was abandoned, he approached. A quick search turned up nothing of interest. He still had no cell reception. The cops should find the vehicle and hopefully, follow.

He located the trail where the group had moved off on foot, still heading in a an easterly direction, toward the Mt. Hood National Forest. This puzzled him. *Why east? Hell, if you think the woods are thick here, wait 'til you see the Hood.* He checked his watch. *Eight hours to sunset. Don't know where they're going but they should only make three-quarters of a mile, maybe a mile an hour. Women will slow them down; maybe not Pat, but Marcie will. I better catch up and slow 'em down some more myself.*

Mase had Flyboy lead them, assuming his sense of direction was better than any of the others. Flyboy did the best he could, but without a compass, it was extremely difficult for anyone except a skilled outdoorsman, hunter, or hiker to maintain a course. He kept detouring around thick tangled underbrush and dense stands of trees. It was inevitable that they would veer in one direction or the other. In general terms, without a directional aid like a compass or landmark, people on foot have a tendency to stray toward their dominant side. Flyboy was right handed so it was not surprising that they veered in a southerly direction. A deep, fast flowing creek with extremely steep banks pushed them even farther south.

The going was tough. Properly attired and outfitted, it would have been easier, but still not easy. The only one with anything close to proper attire was Pat Stallings She was in jeans, plaid shirt, jacket, and sturdy boots. The four men were dressed in slacks, cotton shirts, and street shoes. Marcie was wearing a wool blend pants suit, cotton blouse and two inch heels.

Except for Pat, everyone else's clothes were already looking the worse for wear, as branches and brambles snagged and ripped small bits from shirts and trousers.

Mase called a halt. "How far do you think it is, Flyboy?"

He shrugged. "Hard to tell in this stuff. I'm not even sure we're travelling in the right direction. I *know* we aren't going in a straight line."

"What're you talkin' about?"

"Without a compass or map, it's impossible to maintain the correct heading. All I can do is keep going east – sort of."

"Sort of? What the fuck do you mean sort of? We gotta get to that chopper and you gotta get us there."

"I'm doin' the best I can Mase, but you can't travel in a straight line in this stuff, not without a machete and a bulldozer. It's hard to get a fix on the sun through these trees. We're goin' easterly, at least I think we are, and that's the best I can do. When we hit 224 and find a mile marker, I can get a fix on where we are and then find the chopper. Meantime, we just keep goin' easterly."

The other four were listening with varying degrees of interest. Abe was getting hungry and a little tired from lugging a knapsack full of ammo. Del was getting frustrated from having to push the two women along. Pat was mad and had been trying to get a mental image of where they were in case the opportunity to escape arose. Marcie was frightened, exhausted, and bewildered by this seemingly endless wilderness. She was scratched and bruised from falling and sore from more strenuous walking than she'd ever done in her life.

"All right, we'll take a break here; 10 minutes. Abe, you go on back down our trail for a ways. Keep watch in case someone's following us."

Abe had just sat down and was looking forward to resting. "Aw what fer, Mase? Ain't nobody followin' us."

"What 'fer' is because I said to, now git your ass back down the trail. Move!"

"How far is a ways?"

"I don't know; 50 yards or so."

Grumbling to himself, Abe left his knapsack and did as he was told. Del settled with his back against a tree. Mase and Flyboy did the same.

Pat and Marcie sat side by side in the center of a triangle formed by their kidnappers. Marcie was rubbing her legs to ease the ache. The two women had been silent up to now, but for different reasons.

Pat was watching, looking for a chance to escape. She hoped that her silence would cause the men to pay less attention to her. Marcie had been raised in New York. Her mother had told her from a young age, in situations like this never call attention to yourself. Trying to be invisible was the safest course of action.

Pat was worried about the other woman. She wasn't dressed for this kind of hiking, especially her shoes. She seemed composed and quiet, but Pat had seen the fear and panic that lurked just below the surface.

Marcie leaned close and lowered her voice. "What do you think is going to happen; to us, I mean?"

Pat looked around. No one was paying attention to them. "I don't know. Best thing to do is keep your eyes open and we'll make a run for it if we get a chance." She paused. "I'm Pat Stallings."

"Marcie Watson. Wouldn't it be better to wait for the police?"

"They may not get to us, at least not in time. This isn't the big city. We're a long way from anywhere, right now; finding us is going to take the police a while. We're pretty much on our own I think, for now at least."

"Who do you think it was that shot at us?"

"I don't know." That wasn't true. She was sure she knew who it was.

"The police?"

"I don't think so. They would have called out before they fired and I think they would have hit somebody when they did shoot. Whoever it was used a rifle and they weren't too far away. Pretty hard to miss at that range."

"Why do you think they missed?"

Pat looked to see if any of the gang could hear them. "To get us right where we are now; here instead of out on the road."

"Where do you think they're taking us?"

"They said something about a chopper. I guess they must have a helicopter hidden out here someplace."

"What do you think will happen to us when we get there?"

"I don't know. They'll probably leave us. It wouldn't make any sense taking us along." That isn't what she thought at all.

"You don't think they'd, you know, get rid of us, do you? I mean, we know what they look like."

"So does everyone who was in the bank."

"I guess. That poor man! Why did they shoot him? He wasn't armed and he wasn't doing anything."

"I don't know." Pat decided she needed to change the subject. "You okay?"

She nodded. "My feet hurt and my legs are a bit sore. I'm not used to this kind of walking. I'm more of a sidewalk girl."

"Where are you from?"

"New York."

"How'd you happen to be in a bank in Sholalla? It's a long way from Broadway."

"I was just asking for directions. I was looking for someone."

"Must be someone special to come all that way," Pat observed, curious.

"I only came down from Seattle. I was there on business. Dutch is pretty special. We used to work together. I've got some exciting news for him."

Hearing his name was like an electric shock. "Dutch Yancy?"

Marcie's eyes widened slightly. "Yes. Do you know him?"

Pat nodded but didn't speak. *So **she's** the one!* In all the conversations they'd had, he never actually said the name of the woman that brought (or drove) him to Sholalla. Now, here she was. She looked at Marcie with renewed interest.

"I guess in a small town everybody knows everybody else," Marcie continued.

"Pretty much, yah."

"How do you know, Dutch?"

"I'm the local vet. I hooked him up with his dog."

"Oh yes, he said something about having a dog wolf or wolf dog."

Pat just nodded. Though she looked somewhat disheveled, there was no doubt Marcie was a beautiful woman; high cheekbones, small straight nose, wide set blue eyes, strong chin and a complexion that spoke of minimal exposure to the elements. *I can see the attraction. Hard to compete with that. I wonder why he walked away from her.*

"You and Dutch old friends then?" Pat tried to keep a curious but noncommittal tone.

"We were together almost every day for three years." She frowned. "Why do you ask?"

"No reason. You know how it is; small town, everybody knows everything about everybody else. It's the combined blessing and curse of living in a place like Sholalla."

"God, New York is *so* different. I don't know anything about the people in the next apartment. It took me two years to even learn their name."

"I hear it's like that in big cities." She desperately wanted to find out more about their 'one-sided' relationship, as Dutch termed it.

Dutch was cautious at first, wary of a possible ambush. He was relying heavily on Sasha's extraordinary senses. The longer he followed the more confident he became that the bank robbers weren't expecting anyone to be following them, at least not as close as he was. He gradually increased his speed until he was moving through the bush at a fairly quick pace – faster than the group ahead of him. He tried to keep the noise to a minimum, but some noise was unavoidable. Sasha was just ahead of him, following the trail of broken brush and disturbed undergrowth. The dog had Pat's scent and was eagerly trying to catch up to the vet.

Suddenly the dog stopped, crouching. Dutch caught the low sound of a growl, deep in her throat. He put a restraining hand on her shoulders and knelt beside her.

"Good girl," he whispered.

Looking at the direction the trail ran, he moved off until he was a good 30 feet to one side, then moved parallel to the trail. He was careful, moving slowly and quietly. The dog moved with him. When he put a hand on her shoulders, he could feel her quivering with excitement and anticipation.

He had gone about 100 feet when Sasha went to ground and froze. She was looking toward the trail. The hackles on her neck and shoulders were up; a low growl was coming from her throat. Dutch knelt beside her and put his hand on her back to quiet her.

He was unsure how far ahead whatever it was that troubled Sasha, but he was willing to bet it was a some*one* rather than a some*thing*. He crept forward, relying on Sasha to locate the danger. When she began looking off to one side, he knew he was close. When she was looking sideways, he put her in a down and signalled her to stay.

He moved very slowly in the direction Sasha was looking. He looked carefully before moving and only moved a few feet before stopping and looking again. Finally, he saw what he was looking for.

Abe was bored. *What am I gonna see out here in this jungle anyways? How's come it's always me? How's come I always git the shit jobs? What's wrong with Del or Flyboy doin' this shit sometimes? Oh no, it's always Abe, ain't it? This ain't goddamn fair!* Dutch was within two feet of him before he sensed anything was wrong. He didn't have time to turn around before a rifle butt connected with his skull and everything went hazy.

Abe regained consciousness with a headache. He tried to lick his lips but there was some kind of cloth across his mouth. He tried to reach it but his hands wouldn't move. They were tied behind him. He opened his eyes to the most frightening thing he'd ever seen. In front of him, teeth bared, was a dog – or a wolf. He didn't know which and he didn't care. He jerked his head to the side and his throat was stung and ripped by vicious little thorns. A blackberry vine was wrapped around his neck securing him to the tree he was sitting against. His movement caused the animal to issue a low growl and rise to a half crouch. Abe froze, sure his next breath would be his last.

"You're awake," came a man's voice. "Good. Let's talk."

Chapter 9

Even though his entire department was only four full time people, including himself, it took Police Chief Corby Danvers time to organize the pursuit. He dispatched Simon Judd and his cousin Roy Samuels to take up the chase immediately, while he sent Masie Alcott to the bank to take statements and secure the crime scene. He also wanted to know about Maurice Chambers' condition and ensure he was on his way to the ER.

He placed a quick call to the police station in Estacada and asked them to set up a roadblock at the 211/224 intersection. He called the state police and asked them for assistance. Lastly he placed a call to the FBI office in Portland and reported the robbery, shooting, and kidnappings. He called four of his reserve officers and told them to come in and report to Masie. Before he got into his cruiser, Rusty Jacobs came running over and stopped him.

"Not now, Rusty, haven't got time. I have to get after Simon and Roy."

"This is about the robbery, Corby."

"See Masie, she's taking statements."

"Dutch Yancy is after 'em."

Danvers stopped dead in his tracks. "He's what?"

"He's right behind 'em."

"What in the hell does he think he's doing? This is a job for the police. God damn it!"

"I think he's screwing 'em up. They turned in at the old Miller place and tried to swap vehicles and he stopped them."

"He what?"

"He stopped 'em. Parked his van across the drive so they couldn't get out and now they're headed east, cross country toward the Hood. He's behind 'em and he's got that dog of his with him. He said to tell you, you can pick up the trail in the woods behind the Miller place."

"Is he crazy? He's got no business chasin' after armed bank robbers!"

"He's got his rifle and a handgun and he's got that dog, so he isn't exactly unarmed. I think he knows both the hostages."

"Why?"

"Well there's Doc Stallings and it seems like the other woman was askin' directions to his place when they robbed the bank and took her."

Danvers paused. "You stay close to that phone of yours. If he contacts you, you let me know."

"Okay, Chief."

On the way out of town, Danvers checked in with Masie to see if everything was okay and to get any additional details. Maurice was alive, just barely, when they put him in the ambulance. The paramedics didn't seem too hopeful that he'd survive the trip to the ER.

"Hey Del, get that brother of yours and let's go."

"Okay Mase." Del got up and walked back down the trail a few feet. "Abe. Hey, Abe! Come on."

"Go on down and get him. He probably can't hear you through all the trees."

Del walked back down the trail. There was no sign of his brother.

"Abe?"

Silence.

"Abe! Quit screwin' around! Come on, we're leavin'!"

Silence.

"God damn it, Abe, where the fuck are you?" Del was starting to worry. He looked around but couldn't tell just where it was that Abe had been waiting.

Dutch looked at the man sitting tied against the tree. He had stripped the man's shirt and torn it into strips. He used the strips to tie him to the tree. Before he could ask his first question, he heard someone calling.

"They lookin' for you?"

The man didn't answer. He was too busy watching Sasha who gazed at him with an unblinking stare. He was sure she was sizing him up for dinner. He tried to wiggle further away but the tree was in the way.

Dutch grinned. "Don't worry. Sasha is very loyal. She's only part wolf and she only eats when and what I tell her to. I haven't told her to eat anything yet." It was obvious from his expression that the man believed him. He was enjoying the man's discomfort.

"It wouldn't be a good idea for you to shout. It will make her very nervous. She might go for dinner anyway, know what I mean?"

Abe slowly nodded.

"Good. What's your name?"

"Abe." The word came out as a croak.

"Whole name."

"Abner Ross."

"How many of you are there, Abner?"

"Four." He didn't sound quite so croaky now.

"Who are they?"

"There's Mase and Flyboy and Del."

"Last names?"

"Mase is Mase Krilley, I think his first name's Mason. I don't know Flyboy's name. Mase never called him nuthin' but Flyboy. An' Del, that's Delbert Ross. He's my brother."

"And what's the plan, Abner? Where are you guys headed?"

Abe didn't answer. Mase had threatened that if any of them were captured and revealed the plan before the rest got away, he would find them and kill them.

"Come on, Abe, where are you headed?"

Still no answer.

Dutch gave a hand signal to Sasha who rose and moved forward a step. Abe shrank back, trying to get inside the tree.

"Okay, okay! Call that damn thing off!"

"Careful, Abe. Sasha is very sensitive. She doesn't like bad language. It offends her spiritual values. Where are you headed?"

"A chopper in the woods near a highway over east of here somewheres. We're headed for that."

"Where, exactly?"

"I dunno." He looked at the dog, fearful. "Honest to God, mister, I don't know! Flyboy, he flies the thing and he's the only one knows where it is. He stashed it and we picked him up beside the road."

"Which road?"

"A highway; 242."

There are some clearings over there, away from the hiking trails. You might set a small chopper down, camouflage it. It would be okay for a day or two, maybe more. If you get away in a vehicle, no one would look for you to switch to a chopper. Clever.

Dutch listened closely. The shouting had stopped. Either they were busy looking for Abe, or had abandoned him and were moving on.

"What about the hostages? What are you planning on doing with them?"

"I dunno."

"Why drag them through the woods with you? They're slowing you down."

"I dunno." Abe eyed Sasha. "Honest, I don't know. Mase, he said to leave them in the bank but Del, he tole me ta bring 'em. I dunno what they got in mind. Nobody said nuthin' about 'em yet; they don't never tell me nuthin'." Abe was hoping his lie sounded convincing.

Dutch needed to get on with the pursuit. "All right, Abe, here's what I'm going to do. I'm going to take you over to the trail you guys left coming through the brush. The cops will be along in a few hours and they'll pick you up. If I hear any noise, I'll send Sasha back and believe me, you don't want that. Do you understand?"

He gave a subtle hand signal and Sasha stood and took a step forward. She was now only inches from his feet. "Yeah, yeah, I got it, I got it!"

"Oh, one more thing; what does Flyboy look like?"

"Whadda ya mean, ya can't find him?"

"I mean he ain't there. I called and looked an' he ain't there."

"I tole that idiot to go about 50 yards. He knows what 50 yards is, don't he?"

"Yeah, he knows. I walked farther than that; I went, musta been 100 yards, an' nuthin'. He ain't there an' there ain't no sign of him."

"Maybe he got lost."

"Nah. He ain't too bright but even he could see where we come through the brush an' trees. Whadda ya wanna do?"

*Son of a bitch, is **anything** gonna go according ta plan? That shithead! Either he ran off or somebody got him. He wouldn't leave his brother, so somebody musta grabbed him. Can't be the cops, they won't be close to us for at least a couple of hours yet, maybe more. Coulda been an animal. Nah, we'd a heard him scream or somethin'. Maybe it's that Rambo bastard with the van. What the fuck's he doin', anyways? Why's he after us? Ain't his goddamn bank. Shit! Abe had most of the extra ammo in his backpack. Lucky he left it behind.*

"Come on, we're gonna get the hell outta here. We gotta move and fast!"

"Wait a minute! We can't leave Abe." His brother might be a pain in the ass but he was still his brother.

"The hell we can't. You wanna stay and look for him, you go right ahead. We're leavin' an' the money is comin' with us. Flyboy, you grab Abe's pack."

"Come on, Mase. He's my brother."

"That's right, he's **your** brother."

"Hey Mase," interjected Flyboy, "if the cops grab him, he can identify us."

"They had cameras in the bank. They'll identify us anyways. We gotta move an' get to the chopper. The quicker we get outta here, the better. Abe'll hafta take his chances."

More than any of the others, Flyboy wanted to get to the chopper. He wouldn't feel comfortable until he was at the controls and they were in the air. "Come on, Del," he said. "Mase is right. We have to get as far away as we can, as fast as we can. Abe'll be all right. He can avoid the cops in the woods and we can meet up with him later, in Vegas. Come on."

Del hesitated. He loved his brother but he didn't want to go back to prison. Bank robbery, kidnapping, murder; they had a lot to answer for if they got caught. Abe would have to look out for himself!

"Okay, let's go."

Dutch hurried up the trail left by the fleeing group. He found the small clearing where they rested but couldn't tell anything else. He was about to move on when he noticed Sasha sniffing the ground. He looked where she was sniffing and found a small silver concho. He recognized the ornament as one from Pat Stalling's belt. He kidded her about it occasionally. *Okay, Pat, I got it girl. You're okay so far and still with them. Good enough.*

The two policemen were working their way, slowly and cautiously through the woods, following the trail left but the bank robbers. They were used to the woods, but they weren't dressed for it today. They were both hunters, used to following game trails. They were having no trouble tracking their quarry. Knowing one of the gang had shot down the security guard however, increased their caution, but they knew they were liable to come upon Dutch Yancy and his dog first.

"Chief, this is Roy. Come in."

"Go ahead, Roy." The response was crackly and a little weak.

"We're still trackin' 'em. Looks like they probably still got the hostages with 'em. No sign of Dutch or the dog."

"How far behind 'em are you?"

"Don't know, too hard to tell. Sign's fresh but that's all we can tell."

"Okay. You boys stick with it but you be careful. Help is comin', so hang in there."

"Right, Chief. Out."

"I reckon we can move some faster, Roy," said his cousin. "We must be an hour or so behind 'em, don't you think?"

"Probably. Can't figure out where Yancy is. He must be after 'em, but I can't tell."

"Well, if he was right behind 'em, he'd have to be careful about getting ambushed. It was me, I'd stay off to the side somewhere, parallel 'em. He's got that dog, though. Should give him warnin' before he stumbles into anything bad."

"He that smart? His dog that good?""

Simon shrugged. "Dunno; maybe."

"Well, let's pick up the pace, but be careful. Hang back maybe 20, 30 feet. No sense both of us getting' shot."

"Danvers to base, come in."

"This is base," responded Masie Alcott, "go ahead, Chief. Over"

"Masie, I want you to get me everything you can on Dutch Yancy, especially any military records. Over"

"Sure, Chief. Any particular reason? Over."

"Yes. How's Maurice? Over."

"No word yet. Over."

"How much did they get?"

"Haven't got the final figures, but it looks like about $70,000. Over."

"Okay. Keep me posted and let me know as soon as you get that information on Yancy. Danvers out."

"Roger that. Base out."

Moving on the trail, Dutch knew he was close, so he moved picked up his pace. Sasha ranged ahead of him, alert, stopping periodically to sniff the air or ground. He jogged when he could, stopping frequently to listen. He was rewarded when he finally heard the sounds of breaking branches. They couldn't be more than 40 yards or so ahead of him.

He wasn't sure how close to Highway 224 he was. It was too hard to tell without a map and compass. He was sure they were headed in an easterly direction, but the trail seemed to be veering south. He was worried that they might be getting close to the helicopter. He had to slow them down somehow, and quickly.

Chapter 10

The underbrush was getting thicker. It was harder to push through the wooded areas because there were more fallen trees and branches to entangle their feet. Marcie was having a difficult time and Mase was continually snarling at both women to pick up their pace. After an hour they stopped again. The men were getting tired and Marcie was exhausted. Pat Stallings was coping with the trek better than any of the others.

"I don't know how much longer I can keep going, Pat." There were red welts on Marcie's face and hands, and her jacket and trousers were torn in several places. Her shoes were starting to come apart as well.

Pat sat next to her, back against a large pine. "Hang in there, Marcie. It won't be long now."

"How do you know? I don't think even they know where this helicopter is."

"I'm not talking about the helicopter."

"What do you mean?"

Pat looked to see if any of the men could hear her. Lowering her voice, she said, "I don't think Abe just walked off. Someone is following us and I think they grabbed him."

"Who? The police?"

Pat shook her head. "No. It's Dutch."

"Dutch?" Marcie's voice was raised.

"Shhh! Be quiet." When she looked, Mase had turned and was watching them. She remained silent until he looked away.

"I recognized his van at the farm. He was the one that took those shots at us. I'm pretty sure he's still behind us and I think he's the one that got Abe."

"Dutch? Are you sure? Where did he learn to do this kind of stuff?" She had a hard time equating the man she remembered in New York from the person Pat was talking about.

"I don't know. He does know these woods. He's been cutting wood here for years." She paused and looked at Marcie. "You were with him for what, three years? Did he ever tell you what he did before he worked for you?" Marcie didn't answer right away. "Marcie?"

"He never talked about that." She wore a strange expression as she said it.

"What did you talk about?"

"Work and . . . . ."

"And?"

Marcie frowned. "Me. If it wasn't work, we talked about, ... me." She paused. "He was very good that way. He listened and always turned the conversation to me, what I thought, what I was doing, all about *my* past. He never talked about himself."

"Did you ever ask him?"

Again she paused before answering. "No, I never did." Her expression struck Pat as the perfect example of a person having an epiphany. After a moment, Marcie said again, very quietly, "I never did."

Her expression changed and Pat saw sadness and regret. "I was an awful idiot, Pat. Dutch was right in front of me all the time and I was so caught up in my work and chasing, . . I don't know, success, a dream, something, I just didn't pay any attention. I think he was in love with me and I didn't even see it so he left. They say it's never too late, if you really love someone. I hope that's true." Pat felt a sinking sensation in her stomach. She had a feeling she was going to lose Dutch before she even had time to figure out how she felt about him.

Sasha froze in her tracks and crouched. Dutch moved up and knelt beside her. "Good girl," he said quietly. Motioning her to 'stay', he moved forward, quietly, cautiously. He was about to move around a thick stand of shrubs when he heard someone talking.

"So how far do you think, Flyboy? We can't stay in these woods forever and if somebody spots the chopper, we're screwed. You parked the goddamned thing; how far away is it?"

"I told you, Mase, I don't know. Without a map, I'm not sure where the hell we are. If we keep going east, we should hit Highway 242. Once we get there I can see a mile marker. I'll know exactly where we are and how far it is to the chopper, but first we gotta get to the highway."

"That son of a bitch with the van! I swear to Christ, if I ever run into him, I'm gonna beat him to death."

"This is all bullshit," said Del. "We shoulda gone after the bastard at the farm. There's only one a him and four of us, or at least there was. We coulda got him. Instead, here we are, wanderin' around in this damn jungle, lost, an' getting' *more* lost every goddamn minute; *and* we lost Abe." His tone was getting more and more contemptuous. "Great job, Mase. Hell of a mastermind you turned out ta be."

Mase looked at him. "First off, you dumb bastard, this ain't no jungle. You wouldn't recognize a jungle if you were in one."

"This ain't no jungle," mimicked Del. "Glad you recognize what's important!"

Mase got slowly to his feet. "Listen, shit-for-brains, you came to *me*, remember? You wanted in on the job. You thought that hitting a small town first to try it out, see how well the plan would work, you thought it was a *great* idea. Well we did, and it didn't work out, so tough shit! We're here now and coulda, woulda, shoulda don't mean shit. We deal with what is, the way it is. You want to got it alone, take off, go ahead, fine by me, but the money stays with me. If you're stayin', shut the fuck up unless you got something helpful to say. I got enough on my mind without listenin' to you bitch and moan."

"Do ya? Do ya really? You figured a way to get us outta here? You figured a way to get us somethin' ta eat?"

"Shut up, Del! Just shut the hell up."

The overheard exchange caused Dutch to smile. He backed slowly and silently away from the bushes and made his way back to the waiting animal.

"Well, well; trouble in paradise," he whispered. "Come on Sasha, time to have some fun."

He moved away from the trail for 10 yards, then turned and moved parallel to it, making as little noise as possible. The thickness of the undergrowth made one way as good as another when it came ease of passage. He worked his way around the group, then cut back toward their position.

When he estimated he was directly in the path of their direction of travel, he looked for a place to wait. There were several thickets across a small clearing. He chose the leftmost one and settled down to wait.

Simon Judd froze in his tracks, one foot poised to take a step. He eased his foot down and crouched low. He signalled Roy to come up and join him.

"What is it?"

"Somebody's out there. *This is Officer Simon Judd! Come out with your hands up!*"

"I can't. I'm tied up. I can't move," came the response.

The two policemen looked at each other. "Could be a trick. Cover me, Sy. I'll check it out."

"Be careful. I don't want to be explainin' nuthin' to your mama."

Roy gave him a grin and started cautiously forward. Simon waited, tense and worried. After what seemed like an hour, Roy called out to him, "Come on up, Sy; it's okay. Seems we got an early Christmas package, all gift wrapped and everything."

A few minutes later, Simon was on the radio with Chief Danvers. "Hey Chief, you won't believe this; Yancy left us a present. Over."

"What are you talking about? Over."

"Left us one of the bank robbers all tied up in a neat package. Tried to tell us he was a victim but when we get him back, I'm pretty sure the people who were in the bank will identify him. I read him his Miranda anyway. Says his name's Abner Ross. Mean anything to you? Over."

"No. Where are you?" Simon gave him their GPS co-ordinates. "Can you leave him there and continue after the suspects? Over."

"I'm not sure that's a good idea, Chief. I'm not too worried about the bears, but a mountain lion might find him pretty tasty." Simon winked at his cousin while Abe's eyes grew wide in alarm.

"Hey, wait a minute! You can't *leave* me here. Come on! I'm in custody. You gotta protect me."

"Hey Chief, Abner says we gotta protect him. That right? Over"

"You mean like he protected Maurice?"

"How's he doin'? Over."

"He's out of surgery. Doctors say he's got a fighting chance. You go ahead, follow the trail. I'll tell the county boys to pick him up on the way in after you. Leave him in the middle of the trail so they can find him. Over."

"Okay Chief. Simon out." He turned to Roy. "Help me get him up and over to the trail. Chief says leave him there for the county guys to pick up. Probably better handcuff him around a tree."

"Hey, wait a minute! What about them mountain lions?" Abe was starting to panic at the prospect of being left again.

"Aw hell, don't worry, Abe. You just be real quiet and they might pass you by, . . . maybe, . . . if they've just eaten. If one of 'em does stop, it's not a terrible big problem; they only eat a little at a time, so you should survive until the county guys find you. 'Course you might be missin' some bits, but probably won't be anything important."

Simon and Roy continued on the trail, leaving the protesting Abe sitting handcuffed to a tree alongside the trail. Once they were out of earshot, Roy said, "That was really nasty, don't you think, letting him think there were mountain lions around here."

"He deserves it. They shot Maurice."

Dutch watched the brush in front of him carefully. There was one spot where the undergrowth was not quite as thick and he expected them to come through that way. Beside him, Sasha was standing alertly, ears pointed forward.

"Come on, let's go! We gotta move."

Pat looked up. "Can't we rest a while longer? She's worn out and she isn't dressed for this kind of hiking."

"Ain't none of us dressed for this kinda hiking." He paused. "Maybe you're right; maybe she should stay here and rest – permanently." With a nasty smile, he pointed his AK-47 at the sitting Marcie.

Pat stepped in front of her. "Wait a minute!" She turned to help Marcie up.

"That's what I thought. Amazing what you can do when you're given a little incentive. I gotta keep that in mind for later. Now *move*!" The women followed after Mase and Flyboy. Del brought up the rear. He kept turning around and looking behind him, unsure of who or what, if anything, was following them.

Chief Danvers had just finished radioing Abe's co-ordinates to the county authorities when the radio came to life. "Base to Chief. Come in. Over."

"This is Danvers, Masie; go ahead. Over."

"Chief, I got that information on Dutch Yancy. Over."

"Okay Masie; go ahead. Over."

Five minutes later, he was replacing the mic in his cruiser. *Jesus, I was worried about Yancy. I better start worrying about the suspects. They stepped into a world of hurt when he went after 'em.*

Mase was coming around a large tree when a bullet hit the trunk inches from his head, followed instantly by the loud crack of a rifle shot at close range. He immediately ducked behind the tree and went down on one knee. He brought the AK-47 up to his shoulder and fired a burst at what he thought was the source of the shot. Behind him, Flyboy was crouching on the trail while Del had also taken cover behind a tree. Marcie screamed as Pat pulled her to the ground.

There was a deafening silence after the shots. Mase knew the shot had come from somewhere ahead but he couldn't pinpoint the location. *Cops or is that him? How in the hell did he get* **ahead** *of us?* He waited but there was no other sound. He was unsure about the location of the shooter. Even the birds had stilled their background music in response to the shot.

The rounds from Mase's burst went over his head. Dutch immediately moved to his right along the line of thickets and signalled Sasha to follow. He moved about 25 feet and stopped where he had a view of the tree Mase was sheltering behind. He could see part of Mase's right side and sighted in on his arm. He had a clear shot.

"Mase!" he shouted out.

"Whadda ya want?" shouted Mase. He was surprised when the voice came from the left.

"Let the women go." After he spoke, Dutch moved again to his right, another 20 feet. There was no response from Mase. Dutch knelt and pushed the rifle slowly through the thicket. Mase had inched around the tree but Dutch could still see part of his left side.

Mase was slowly raising his AK-47 and pointing it toward the thicket when Dutch fired again. The bullet nicked the tree just a couple of inches from Mase's shoulder. He immediately scooted around in an attempt to put the tree between himself and the unseen sniper. *Where the hell is that son of a bitch? Is he movin' or is there more than one of him out there?*

Dutch scrambled back to his original location. He could see all of Mase's body now and he threw another shot into the tree. He moved again, back to a spot a few yards beyond the place where he fired the second shot.

"If you want to get to your chopper, let the women go."

Mase didn't respond. He was busy signalling to Del. When he got his attention, he motioned to him to move around and flank the unseen shooter. Del nodded his understanding and started off to his leftt, through the trees and brush, keeping as low as possible.

"This might be our chance to get away," Pat whispered to Marcie. The look she received in return was full of fear. Marcie was rooted to the spot.

"Sssst, Flyboy!" When the man looked at him, Mace said, in a low voice, "You keep an eye on them." He motioned toward the women. "If they make a break for it, shoot 'em!"

Dutch heard him speak but didn't catch the words. He caught a fleeting glimpse of movement, ahead and to the right. *Trying to flank me.* He touched Sasha to get her attention, motioned her to follow him, and moved back toward his original position. He passed it and kept going, beyond the line of shrubs, moving into the undergrowth as quickly and quietly as possible.

"Wait a minute. Let's talk about this," Mase called out.

Ignoring him, Dutch kept going. After 20 yards or so, he moved to his forward quickly, hopeful that they would be concentrating on where he *had* been, not where he *was*. When he figured he'd gone far enough, he moved to his rightt again until he found the trail Mase had made. He moved carefully up the trail until he caught sight of something bright red ahead of him. It was Pat's plaid shirt.

"Hey, come on! We can make a deal!"

Del moved carefully through the undergrowth toward the line of shrubs. At the same time, Dutch was moving closer, Sasha right beside him. He could see Pat through the low branches and brush. She was on the ground, Marcie beside her. He was about to step closer when a movement caught his eye. He froze, thankful he was wearing a dark green jacket.

Slowly another figure came into view, moving across his line of sight. He recognized Flyboy from the description Abe had given him. Somewhere ahead of Flyboy was Mase while Del was working his way around to flank his old position.

Easing his rifle up, he sighted carefully and fired. The bullet kicked up dirt and took off a small piece of the sole of Flyboy's boot. Flyboy fell and scrambled for cover. Dutch fired again, just a foot from Flyboy's hair.

"Move again and the next one won't miss!" he called. Flyboy froze. "Mase, let the women go or you won't need the chopper; you won't have a pilot to fly it."

"Shoot him and I'll kill 'em both!" shouted Mase, swinging his weapon to cover the two women.

That other bastard will be trying to sneak up on me. I got about 10 minutes, maybe less. "I'll make you a deal, Mase. Let the women go and you can walk away. If you don't, or if you hurt them, you all die; you, Del, and Flyboy here. You got two minutes and then I start shooting. Flyboy will be first."

"Come on, Mase, he's got us cold. Let's just take the money and get out of here." Flyboy tried to speak quietly but Dutch could hear every word.

"Shut up! Lemme think."

Dutch kept glancing at Sasha. He was depending on her sense of hearing and smell to warn when Del was getting close. They were downwind of the group, so he should get plenty of warning. He glanced at his watch. *One minute thirty left.*

He looked at the group ahead of him. Pat and Marcie were looking in his direction. Flyboy was turned away, looking in Mase's direction. He took a chance and moved from the protection of the tree and large bush, across the trail to another tree. The concealment wasn't as good but he had a better view. He was hoping Pat had seen him. *One minute.*

He looked around. Behind him was a large area of chain ferns. Some of them were seven feet tall. *Thirty seconds.*

"Thirty seconds, Mase. What's it gonna be?"

Mase looked at the trio behind him. "Bring her here," he said in a low voice, pointing to Marcie.

"Come on, Mase. Give him the women."

Mase shifted his weapon to point at Flyboy. "Bring her!"

Flyboy moved closer to the women and reached for Marcie's arm. She drew back. He stretched his hand out and Dutch fired, hitting him in the upper arm. The impact knocked him down. Flyboy screamed and grabbed his arm, dropping his weapon in the process.

"Next one kills him, Mase."

"Flyboy! You all right?" called Mase.

"It's my arm. It's broken!"

Dutch moved back to the concealment of the ferns, signalling Sasha to join him. He moved into the ferns for only a few feet. It was enough to achieve concealment. He couldn't see the women or Flyboy now, but that didn't concern him. He was more worried about Del. He was moving toward, but he wasn't sure now from which direction. He crouched, waiting, hand on Sasha's back. The dog was quivering with excitement.

For several minutes there was no movement or sound except the occasional moan coming from Flyboy as he clutched his wounded arm. It was bleeding heavily, the blood soaking his shirt sleeve as it journeyed toward his wrist. The women were huddled together, frightened. Mase was looking in the direction of the shot, his eyes searching for evidence of the shooter. Del was retracing his steps to try and approach the shooter from another angle.

Dutch and Sasha waited quietly in the shelter of the ferns.

"You hear that?" queried Simon from his place ahead.

"What?" asked Roy.

"I thought it sounded like a shot."

"I didn't hear anything."

"Wait a minute. Listen."

Both men stood still, straining their ears. After a full minute, Simon said, "Ears must have been playing tricks on me."

"Why don't you take a break. I'll take point for a while," offered Roy.

"Okay. Careful."

Roy moved past him and continued up the fresh track through the brush.

The first tendrils of desperation were beginning to wrap themselves around Mase's brain. *This guy just won't let go. He's like a dog with a bone; he's grabbed ahold of **us** won't let go. The only way to get rid of him is to kill him, or at least disable him. That'll take time; time I ain't got!*

That wasn't the way he liked to do things. He'd been taking things that didn't belong to him from people and places, mostly places, for as long as he could remember. He'd gotten away with it mostly, except for a couple of short stretches in jail, for a very long time ago. Sometimes people got hurt; occasionally somebody died, like today, but never on purpose.

That goddamned imbecile! What the fuck did he shoot the old man for? **And** *take the women? I know what he thinks is gonna happen later, with the women, but he's fulla shit. We ain't addin' rape to the list. Christ, about the only capital crimes left are treason, sedition and espionage! I ain't* **never** *gonna work with anybody I don't know again! Never! Goddamn amateurs!*

Snaking his way backwards, Mase crawled to the trio huddled together on the ground. Flyboy was clutching his arm and moaning. Marcie was watching the blood in frozen fascination, unable to do more than breathe and blink. Pat was looking behind her intently, trying to see where Dutch was.

Mase grabbed a handful of Pat's hair and pulled her head back while he pressed his pistol against her neck. "I don't wanna shoot you lady, but if your boyfriend back there shoots again, you're gonna die."

"He's not my boyfriend!"

"Then he oughta be. Come on, get up!" He rose slowly, forcing Pat to her feet, using her as a shield.

"Get up, Flyboy. Use her as a shield. He won't shoot if you stay close enough to her. We'll back outta here, nice and slow. Come on."

Flyboy was in too much pain to argue. Retrieving his pistol and stuffing it into his belt, he grasped a handful of Marcie's jacket and got clumsily to his feet. He pulled Marcie up with him and kept her between him and the place he thought the shot had come from.

Pat's eyes were watering from the pain of Mase's grip on her hair. She kept stumbling as she was pulled along backwards. Keeping her footing was almost impossible when she couldn't see where she was going. Each time she started to fall, his grip on her hair held her painfully upright. Marcie was numb as she felt herself being pulled along after Flyboy. He had a grip on the collars of her jacket and blouse and she stumbled along behind him, struggling to stay upright.

Once they passed the large tree where Mase had been sheltering, and he thought they had some cover, he released his grip on Pat. He moved over to Flyboy and Marcie.

"We should be okay here for a minute. How's your arm?"

"Still bleeding but I guess it's not broken. Hurts like hell though."

"You," Mase turned and nodded at Pat, "Come over here and take a look at his arm. Bandage it up, stop the bleeding. You," he spoke to Marcie, "sit there and don't move." He turned to look back in the direction they'd come.

He coulda killed Flyboy but he didn't. How come? He must be afraid if he kills one of us, I'll kill one of the women. Once she gets him bandaged we'll bug outta here. Del can take care of Rambo and catch up. Maybe Rambo'll take care of him. While they're at it, we should be able to stretch our lead. Maybe they'll take care of each other and solve all my problems.

He smiled at the last thought and turned back to see what was happening. Pat examined the wound and found the bullet had passed through. It missed the bone and, although it was oozing steadily, the blood wasn't pumping out, so the major artery had also been missed. She tore the sleeve off of Flyboy's shirt and ripped off Marcie's jacket pockets. She used the pockets as pads to put over the holes where the bullet had entered and exited. She wrapped the shirt sleeve around his arm and tied it off. The blood continued to seep through, but very slowly. She was fairly sure the major artery was undamaged but she thought she remembered there was a secondary artery somewhere close to where the bullet passed. The bullet may have nicked the secondary. If so, he could still loose a significant amount of blood unless the blood loss stopped. She felt far more comfortable with animal anatomy.

"All right, get up. We gotta move and fast. You," he spoke to Marcie, "better keep up or you won't be walkin' outta here at all. You understand?" Marcie just looked at him, wide eyed. "Do you understand, goddamn it?" he shouted. She nodded dumbly. He didn't ask Pat about the wound and she didn't say anything.

"What about Del?" asked Flyboy.

"He can catch up once he finishes off John Wayne back there."

"What if he doesn't?"

"Then he won't *be* catchin' up. Come on!"

"Look Mase, why don't you get smart?" Pat said. "Leave Marcie behind; whoever is behind us will stop and question her. Then they'll have to take care of her. It will all take time and that'll buy you more time."

He looked at her, searching her face for some sign of subterfuge. *That's an idea. Might do that later. Let's see how much she slows us down and how Del makes out.* "Come on," he snarled, "I ain't wastin' any more time!"

Dutch was still kneeling in the ferns. He wasn't worried about the fugitives getting away. They had to break trail and combined with their lack of knowledge of the forest and an obvious lack of woodcraft, plus the women, would significantly slow their progress. He and Sasha could easily catch up. At the moment he was worried about the flanker. He wasn't sure where he went when he reversed direction. The last shot would draw him back, but from where? Best to wait and see what Sasha picked up.

After 30 minutes, he felt he could wait no longer. He wasn't sure what happened to the flanker; maybe he'd given up and rejoined the party. He hadn't heard him and Sasha hadn't given any sign she heard or smelled him. He couldn't let them get too big a lead. He had to move now.

He got up slowly, quietly. Crouching low he moved carefully to the edge of the ferns and waited, listening. He heard nothing and saw nothing. He slowly stood up and stepped out of the ferns. He never heard the shot. There was a sharp blow to his head and everything went black.

Chapter 11

"Hey Mase, hold up. Did you hear that? It was a shot." Flyboy stopped and pulled Marcie to a stop in front of him.

"Yeah, I heard it. Keep moving," Mase said from behind him.

"That might have been Del, taking care of the guy."

"And it might have been the guy, taking care of Del. Either way, keep moving."

"Shouldn't we wait, in case it's Del, so he can catch up?"

"No. Now move."

"But what about Del?"

"What about him? Look Flyboy, either he's okay, or he's not. Either he catches up, or he doesn't. If he catches up, we split the money three ways; if he doesn't, it's 50-50. That's it."

"That's pretty cold blooded."

"Yeah? Well, it's a cold blooded world, Flyboy. Ain't nobody gonna take care a you, but you. Now let's get movin'."

Flyboy wasn't about to argue. They were going on and that was that. Flyboy was pushing Marcie ahead of him. Mase had taken off his belt and looped it through two of the belt loops on Pat's jeans. He was using it as a leash to pull her along behind him.

Pat kept looking behind her, hoping against hope that Dutch was all right. She couldn't believe he'd followed them. It was so, . . . unexpected.

In all the time she'd known him, she'd never seen anything that hinted he was capable of this. Why? Why would he chase after them, armed bank robbers, killers, for all anyone knew? She looked over at Marcie. *It must be for her. He's doing it for her. He must be. He still loves her and he's trying to save her. Whatever there was between them in New York, he never got over it; now he's trying to save her. She doesn't know it, but as soon as she makes her play for him, he'll tell her. Then what?* She felt a tug at her waist and she stepped off after Mase.

There was a pounding someplace and the sound was driving through his head like a spear. He tried to open his eyes but they wouldn't work. He tried to lift his head but the movement caused so much pain he stopped. *I don't know what happened but I don't want it to happen again – **ever**.*

After a moment, he slowly moved his hand and gingerly put it to his forehead. It didn't help the pounding but it didn't make it any worse either. *So far, so good. I can move something.* He ran his hand over his head and felt something wet and sticky. He used this other hand to slowly touch, then rub his eyes. When he opened them, the light hurt. He blinked and slowly got used to the brightness. He could see the blurry image of something above him. He kept blinking to clear his vision while he explored his head with both hands.

When the ferns above him came into focus, he looked at his hands and saw blood. For a moment, he didn't understand. *What happened? Where did this, . . . oh shit! I've been shot! The son of a bitch shot me! Am I alive? Must be. Why am I still alive? Where's Sasha?*

He slowly raised his head, gritting his teeth and ignoring the increased spikes of pain that caused bright flashes to spark in his vision. He lifted himself into a sitting position, using one hand to brace himself and the other to explore the crease that ran along the side of his head. *Not by much, you bastard; you didn't miss by much. Why didn't you finish me? Where's Sasha?*

Slowly he rolled to his hands and knees. Before he could get his feet under him, there was a rush of sound and a high pitched whine as Sasha came rushing to his side. He put out a hand and felt the rough bristles of her hair while she whined and licked his face.

"All right girl, steady." He pushed her back slightly, then slowly, carefully, his head pounded by at least a dozen jackhammers, Dutch got to his feet. He felt dizzy and fought to keep his balance while nausea in waves washed over him. When it passed, he took a deep breath and slowly raised his head. He had the fleeting thought that he was being stupid, standing up that way, in plain sight. Then it occurred to him; Sasha was here and she wouldn't be if there was any danger.

He took the red bandana from his back pocket and used it to dab along his wound. When he looked at it, there was some blood, but not as much as he expected. The blood flow must have nearly stopped. He used the bandana as a makeshift bandage and tied it around his head. He'd have to wait until he came to a stream to wash.

He stepped out of the ferns. Sasha moved ahead of him, then stopped and turned to look at him. He followed her and she led him to a spot in the brush about 30 yards away. She stopped and sat, waiting for him. When he got up to her, he saw what she wanted him to look at.

On the ground was the bloodied and barely recognizable figure of Delbert Ross. His face was torn and bloody. There was a gaping bloody wound where his throat had been. An AK-47 lay a few feet from his body. Sasha had made sure he didn't finish the job. The dog looked back and forth, from the corpse to Dutch. She whined and shifted her weight. He knelt beside her and put his hand on her head.

"Good girl. You did well, Sasha. Good girl."

The dog leaned against him and gave a low, pleasant growl.

"You know you did well, don't you?" He ruffled her fur.

He picked up the AK and gave the body a quick pat down for spare magazines. He found only one extra 30 round mag. He pocketed it and slung the AK-47 over his shoulder.

"Come on, Sasha. Leave it."

He stood up and immediately regretted it. He'd moved too fast and started a new round of pounding in his head. *Easy does it, easy does it!*

He waited until the pounding eased before he moved back to the ferns to retrieve his rifle. He moved to the place where he'd last seen the group and on to the tree where Mase had sheltered. *How long was I out? I wonder how far ahead of me they are. They must have headed across the clearing and around the thickets. Left or right end?* He wasn't sure.

Sasha was looking up at him, waiting for direction. *This isn't a 'Lassie Come Home' movie; I can't tell her to 'Go find Timmy'. I don't know if she can track or not.* Tracking was not something he'd worked on with the dog. But Sasha did know Pat.

"Go ahead, Sasha," he said, and motioned ahead. "Go ahead."

Sasha took a tentative step or two and stopped to look at him. "Good girl. Go ahead." Again he waved his arm forward. This time the dog put her nose to the ground and began to sniff. She caught the scent. He hoped it wasn't a deer or rabbit.

He followed the dog across the clearing and around the right hand side of the row of bushes. She paused, looked up and around, then put her head down and continued on. As they entered a stand of trees, he saw several fallen branches that had been disturbed recently. It was the right track.

The shadows were lengthening. It had been almost six hours since the robbery and five hours since the two policemen had entered the woods.

"Simon to Base, Simon to Base, come in. Over."

"Simon, this is Base, over."

"Hey Masie. Gonna be dark in a couple of hours. What's the Chief want us to do, over?"

"Wait one. Over."

"How far you figure we are from 242, Sy?" asked Roy.

"Dunno. We been veering south. I'd guess it's a good hour and a half, maybe two hours if we head straight for it."

"Hope the chief calls us in. We ain't exactly equipped for a night out in the woods. 'Sides, I'm hungry. We missed lunch and we're gonna miss dinner too, at this rate."

"Yeah, but Dutch and the guys he's after ain't in any better shape than we are."

"Base to Simon, over."

"This is Simon, over."

"Chief says you might as well come on in, over."

"Okay Masie. Listen, we're closer to the 242 than we are if we backtrack. Can someone come out and pick us up when we get there, over?"

There was a pause. "Chief says sure, just call and give me a mile marker and I'll come get you, over."

"Thanks, Maze. See ya later. Simon out."

"Suppose you'll be wantin' to sit up front with your sugar on the ride back," said Roy.

"Damned right."

"Can't understand why she went for somebody like you when she coulda had a good lookin' fella like me."

"Taste Roy, plain and simple good taste," Simon said, grinning. Roy threw a stick at him as they started off.

"God damn it Flyboy, how far is this highway. It's gonna be dark in a couple three hours."

"I told you a dozen times, I don't know. I didn't know then and I don't know now. I fly planes and helicopters. I use GPS, maps, compasses. You see any of those things around here?"

"Don't be a smart ass!"

"Then don't ask me the same dumb question over and over. At least with the shadows I can be sure we're going east but I don't know how far we have to go."

The group was stopped for another break. They were moving slower as Marcie grew more tired and found it increasingly difficult to walk as her shoes disintegrated. Right now they were only together because Pat had torn strips from her jacket and tied them onto her feet. Flyboy was slowing also as he grew progressively weaker.

Marcie's clothes were showing signs of hard travel, torn and holed in several places by trees and brush. Her entire body was aching, especially her legs. She had never walked so far before and never in such wilderness.

"Come on, let's move."

Marcie looked up, exhausted. "Please, just a little longer. I can't walk much farther without some rest."

"Get on your feet. We wasted too much time already."

"I can't. I need to rest for a little bit more."

Mase stood and looked down at the exhausted women. "Either you get up now, or I'll shoot you where you sit and leave you for the scavengers." His expression said he was deadly serious.

"Then you better shoot both of us." Pat was as surprised as Mase when she spoke. "I'm not moving without her. You'll have to shoot us both and you don't want to do that."

"What makes you so sure, lady? I don't give a shit about either one a you."

"But you do care about a murder charge. This is a death penalty state. Right now you don't know whether the man that was shot in the bank is dead or not. He may have survived. That's only attempted murder and you're only an accessory since you didn't pull the trigger. Shoot us and it's murder, and first degree murder at that. When word gets out that you murdered helpless hostages, you won't ever make it to jail. I'd think about that."

He knew she was right as soon as she said it. He just hated to admit it. *She's got some kinda balls, that one. Reminds me of Vera, a little.* "Awright, 10 more minutes, but then we move, even if you gotta carry her."

Mase turned away in foul temper. Flyboy sank back against a tree, thankful for the additional rest. His arm was getting worse; the pain was now affecting his arm from shoulder to wrist. He was feeling weaker and more tired.

Pat moved next to Marcie. "Here, put your legs up here and I'll give you a massage. Might help for a little while."

Marcie smiled gratefully. "Thank you, Pat, and thank you for what you did. Will he really shoot me?"

"I don't know. It depends on how desperate he is. He knows what I said is true so I think we're okay as long as we keep moving."

"I'll try. It's just that my feet hurt and my legs are so tired and sore. I'm not used to this."

"None of us are." She lowered her voice. "I don't think *they're* doing all that well either. Hang on to that thought." She smiled at Marcie.

"Pat, do you think Dutch is all right? I mean, that shot . . . ."

"I don't know, Marcie. Del hasn't caught up with us yet and that's a good sign. He's a nasty piece of work and I feel better now that he's gone."

Marcie was quiet for a moment, enjoying the relief the massage was bringing her tired limbs. "Pat, why is Dutch doing this? Why is he following us and taking the chance of getting hurt or . . . ." She couldn't bring herself to finish the sentence.

"I don't know. I suppose he doesn't want anything to happen to you and he's going to do whatever he can to prevent you getting hurt."

Marcie looked at her. "What about you?"

"Me?" Pat was surprised. "What about me?"

"Maybe you're the reason."

"Whatever gives you that idea? I'm just the local vet."

"Are you friends?"

Pat hesitated before answering, the memory of the kiss suddenly fresh in her mind. *Is Marcie jealous?* "We've known each other pretty much since he came here so I guess you could say we're friends – sort of. Are you friends with your vet?"

"I don't have any pets." Pat wasn't surprised. Marcie didn't seem like a pet kind of person.

Roy was in the lead when they found Del's body. "Jesus! Simon, come up here!"

Simon hurried forward and skidded to a stop when the saw the body. "What the hell?"

"Who is it? What was it tore him up like that?" asked Roy.

"I dunno. I think he must be one of the bank robbers."

"Yeah but, . . ."

"Dutch has his dog with him, doesn't he? He usually does."

"They said he did. We better call this in."

"Simon to Base, over."

"Base, go ahead, over."

"Maze, we got us a body out here, over."

"Any idea who it is, over?"

"Might be one of the bank robbers. Hard to tell. He's tore up pretty bad, over."

"Okay. What's the location, over?"

Simon checked his GPS and gave the co-ordinates. "What do you want us to do, over?"

There was a long pause. "Chief says wait with the body. He'll have somebody get to you as soon as he can, over."

"He wants us to stay out here all night? Over?"

Chief Danvers voice came over the radio. "Light a fire and sit tight. I'll have somebody from county come in from the 242 or get a chopper in there if they can. Shouldn't take more that a couple of hours."

"Chief, we ain't really equipped for a night out in the woods, ya know? We ain't had nuthin' to eat since breakfast and no water neither. Can you hurry them county boys up, over?"

"I will. Cheer up; you boys are getting overtime for this you know, over."

"Chief, I'm having some very unkind thoughts about what to do with that overtime money right now, over."

"You don't want it?"

"I didn't say that. Just hurry those county boys up, will ya please? Over."

"Roger that. Base out."

Simon looked at Roy. "Shit," he said, which pretty well summed it up.

Chapter 12

Chief Corey Danvers hadn't had a moment to himself since the robbery. Between the pursuit, the news media, the hospital, the mayor and town council, it seemed everyone expected him to have all the answers when he felt like he knew less than everybody else. Besides that there was keeping the county, state and federal agencies informed of what was going on and getting what information they had, which was less than he had. He was grateful when Masie Atwell brought him a cup of coffee and asked, "How you holding up, Chief?"

"Thanks Masie. I'm okay, just haven't had a minute to think, seems like." He sipped the coffee. "At least your boyfriend will be okay, unless that gang doubles back."

Masie looked startled. "My boyfriend?"

Danvers looked amused. "Yeah, Simon Judd; remember him, police officer, tall fella, sandy hair, sorta good lookin' so they tell me?"

"Whatever gave you the idea . . . ."

"Oh for goodness sake, Masie, don't bother to deny it. I'm not blind *or* stupid. Everybody knows you two are sweet on each other. I'm just wonderin' what you're gonna do about it."

Masie turned several shades of red. "Well, you know how the council feels about fraternizing in city service departments, Chief. We both like our jobs, and . . . ."

"You let me worry about the town council."

"Thanks, Chief. Say, that Dutch Yancy turned out to be something. Who'd have guessed?" Masie observed, grateful to change the subject. "I didn't know he was ever in the service."

"He musta been something," observed Danvers. "Marine Corps Force Recon, Navy Cross, Silver Star, Bronze Stars, Purple Hearts. I mean he's a genuine hero. He never said anything about any of it far as I know."

"He's always so quiet and, . . . I don't know, unassuming, I guess."

"The genuine articles usually are. It's the ones with all the 'war stories' that were usually in the rear with the gear."

"You think he's all right? I mean nobody's heard from him or seen him since that last call to Rusty."

"I don't think we have to worry about Dutch Yancy. We should be worrying about whoever he's after. Anything new on Maurice?"

"Hospital says he's holding his own," she replied.

"Any ID on the second hostage?"

"We think we found her car. It's a rental from Seattle. Rental agency says it was rented to a Marcie Watson, New York City address. Picture on her licence matches the CCTV footage from the bank."

"Sounds like it must be somebody from Yancy's past. Case of wrong place at the wrong time, I guess. What does county say about getting some people into Simon and Roy?"

"They'll have a chopper up soon and it should be with them just before dark."

"Okay. You go ahead and get some supper. And can you arrange some kind of relief rotation for the reserve deputies? Tell 'em to get some supper and they can knock off and go home at eight. Should quiet down by then."

"Right, Chief. You want me to bring you something?"

"No thanks. I'll get something later."

Mase started to enter the clearing when he heard the distinctive sound of the approaching helicopter. He froze and motioned behind him for the others to stop. He leaned against a tree and looked up. In a moment the aircraft passed low overhead, the words **SHERIFF'S DEPT** clearly visible on the underside. It came from the direction they were headed and this worried him. He would have to be careful. They were all looking for him; city, county, state, and FBI too. *No one ever said bank robbery was an easy way to make a livin'.*

He looked behind him. Flyboy was leaning against a tree, nursing his arm, looking tired and drawn. The woman he was shepherding looked totally done in. On the other hand, the redhead he had on a leash looked in better shape than anyone, including him. *Says she's a vet but she looks like a part time guide or something. Shoulda pulled the job with **her** instead of the losers I picked! She's just so damn clumsy, always grabbing at tree branches to keep from falling over. Wonder if she's got some kinda ailment.*

"Come on, let's go. We gotta be close to that road by now. Chopper can't be far after that."

"Mase, leave Marcie here," Pat requested again. "She's exhausted and she'll only slow you down. You won't make it if you insist on dragging her along."

"I told you, sister, she's coming. You're all coming. We all make it or **none** of us makes it. Now shuddup about it!"

The pounding had subsided to a dull thumping and the pain was maintaining a steady level as long as he didn't exert himself too much. Sasha was ahead of him, nose to the ground, although he was able to follow the trail pretty well himself. All the broken branches and scuff marks made it fairly easy. It looked like someone was intentionally making the trail easy to follow. Still, as fresh as the tracks were, there was no real way to tell how far behind them he was.

He heard the rapid dull whop-whop-whop of rotor blades before he ever saw the aircraft. It gave him a strange feeling of déjà vu as memories washed through him. He was about to wave but he stopped. *Easy boy. They don't know who you are and that's a good way to get yourself shot. No friendly fire today, thank you very much!*

He reached for his cell phone to try another call to Rusty but he couldn't find it. He couldn't find his .357 either. *Must have lost them when I was hit. Should have realized it was gone. That shot must have scrambled my brain.*

The chopper passed over and he moved on. *They must be moving slower now,* he reasoned. *One of them is wounded and the women would be slowing them down too, at least Marcie would. She isn't dressed for this and she isn't the outdoor type either. She thinks Central Park is a hike in the woods.* He wondered what she made of the forest she was forced to navigate now.

He pushed on after Sasha, who stopped every so often to look back and ensure he was still with her. *I gotta thank Pat for Sasha. I don't think I ever did thank her properly. Best thing that happened to me since I been here.*

He picked up the pace, in spite of the pounding in his head and the pain. *Any dummy could tell which way was east now, from the shadows. Once they get to the highway, they might get away. The women's chances of survival lessen in direct relation to their distance from the highway. No reason to take 'em along once they make it to the chopper. No real reason to let them live either.* This thought spurred him to move faster.

Man, that pilot's got some kinda guts. Simon watched as the pilot set the helicopter down in the small clearing. The tips of the rotor blades just cleared the tree branches. The two policemen had taken numerous pictures and the co-pilot also took pictures as well as a video of the body and surrounding area. They placed Delbert Ross's remains in a body bag and lifted it into the helicopter, then Simon, Roy and the co-pilot climbed aboard.

Simon adjusted his headset and asked the pilot, "You guys see anybody on your way in?"

The pilot shook his head. "Who are we looking for?"

"The bunch that robbed the bank. Should be two men with two women hostages; man and a dog somewhere behind them. See anything like that?"

"Nah. Canopy is too thick and there wasn't anything in any of the clearings that we passed over. We'll take it low and slow on the way back, see if anything shows up. Where we takin' you?"

"Back to Sholalla. There's space to land behind the jail."

"Roger that. Hang on."

Dutch heard the helicopter coming back. He thought it must be using some sort of search pattern to locate the fugitives. It passed on to the northwest.

Mase heard the helicopter coming back and assumed the same thing. He halted everyone under the shelter of the trees. The aircraft continued on its course.

"Helicopter's on its way in," Danvers said to Masie, as she came through the door to the police station. "Simon and Roy are on board and they're bringing in the body they found." He thought Masie looked relieved.

"Are they coming here?"

"Should be here in 10 or 15 minutes."

"What about the guy they found tied up?"

"County boys just picked him up and they're headed back to Miller's farm with him now."

"Two down, two to go. You think Pat and the Watson woman are all right, Chief?"

"We haven't found any other bodies and that's a good sign. I just hope they'll be all right when it gets worse."

"Worse? How can it get worse?"

"They already lost two of their people. Dutch Yancy is behind 'em, state and county boys and maybe the FBI are in front of 'em. When they get squeezed between the two, they'll get desperate. That's when things can go to hell, real quick."

Chapter 13

Mason Krilley's temper had always been his downfall, even as a child. He never considered himself an arrogant, egotistical control freak, yet the few who knew him as anything more than a passing acquaintance would testify that he was all of those things and more. When he made a plan he was sure it was the best plan there could be and he was equally sure no one could possibly think of a better one. Over the years, he had been right – most of the time.

When something went wrong however, or others were not co-operative, he got frustrated. The frustration led to anger; the more frustrated he got, the angrier he became, until he exploded and lashed out irrationally at everyone and everything until his anger burned itself out. He knew this yet was powerless to prevent it, no matter how hard he tried. Right now he was having great difficulty keeping his temper in check.

His plan had been perfect, foolproof. Small banks in small towns; one, two, three, even more in a week. Lie low for a few weeks, then do the same in another state, perhaps even on the other side of the country. Steal a car, rob the bank, in and out quickly; get to the helicopter and disappear. A perfect plan and Sholalla was the test run. It was going like clockwork until Del shot the guard and grabbed the women. Then that John Wayne hero prevented their getaway and forced them to go cross country in these damn woods that never ended. They were lost, or at least not sure where the chopper was, two guys down, a Rambo trailing them, and probably an army of cops in front of them. If they didn't find the chopper soon, they were royally screwed. His perfect plan had turned to crap the moment Del fired that shot and it was getting worse with each passing minute. He was on the brink of losing it.

They had only been moving for 10 minutes and already Flyboy and Marcie were lagging behind. They were crawling along, or so it seemed to Mase, and still those two couldn't keep up. He turned in time to see Marcie stumble and fall, yet again, and that was the last straw. He dropped the belt leash he had attached to Pat and stalked back to the lagging pair. "I told you to keep up, goddamn it! Keep her on her feet and move faster, Flyboy. I ain't gonna tell you again."

"Aw hell, she's worn out, Mase. Cut her loose and leave her here. We still got the other one. We don't need 'em both."

Mase looked down at Marcie, his faced darkening. "You're right, Flyboy. We don't need both of 'em."

Flyboy started to smile, relieved. The smile faded quickly and Mase pulled a switchblade knife from his pocket and bent down toward Marcie. He grabbed her by the hair and pulled her head back.

"Mase, what the fuck are you doing?" Flyboy shouted at him.

Mass turned and snarled at him, "Just what you asked me to do. I ain't gonna waste a bullet, I'm just gonna cut her loose."

Pat watched, frozen in disbelief. Marcie's eyes were open wide, her face a terrified mask. She had both hands wrapped around Mase's wrist. She was so terrified she couldn't even scream.

Flyboy took a step backwards and brought up his pistol, levelling it at Mase. "You ain't gonna kill her, Mase. So help me God, I'll shoot you if you try." He wasn't sure he could; he'd never shot anyone in his life.

They four figures remained frozen, like a tableau in the closing scene of a play. None of them were sure how long they remained locked in place. Then slowly Mase released his grip on Marcie's hair and she sank to the ground. He straightened up and turned to face the other man.

Flyboy didn't know why he did it. He hadn't even thought about it. It was pure instinct. He only knew he couldn't stand by and watch Mase murder the helpless girl. He watched as the expression on Mase's face changed and he grew afraid. He never seen such a look of anger mixed with disbelief in his life. Mase was going to kill him. He knew it as surely as he had ever known anything and he still wasn't sure he could shoot him.

"Mase, I can't let you kill her," he said hurriedly, "not in cold blood like that. I wanna fly us outta here without any more killing. No more. You wanna get away and so do I, but I swear to God, I won't fly if you hurt either one of 'em. You kill 'em if you think **you** can fly that chopper, but I won't fly it if you do."

Slowly the red haze cleared from his mind and Flyboy's words sank in. Mase knew there was still a chance to get to the chopper. Without Flyboy, it would be a useless pile of metal. The chopper was still their best chance to get away. But did they dare leave the woman behind? *She can ID us but so what? Abe's probably singing like a bird right now anyway, and so is Del, if either one of them is still alive. If we get away, it won't matter. We can pull a few more jobs and head for Costa Rica. We can live good down there.* His thinking began to mirror what Pat Stallings had tried to tell him. *If we leave her here, whoever's behind us will have to stop for her. That'll slow him down, give us a better chance. But by God, when we get outta here, I'm gonna straighten Flyboy out so's he'll **never** even **think** about doin' anything like this again.*

Mase looked down at Marcie. "Lady, this is your lucky day. Flyboy, since you worry so much about these women, you grab the other one and let's get outta here. We'll talk about this later."

Flyboy felt weak as relief washed through him. Pat gasped for air, not sure how long she'd been holding her breath. Mase stalked past her and started through the undergrowth, not looking to see if they were following. Marcie began to cry, silently.

Dutch found her 20 minutes later, lying where Mase had left her. When he first spotted her he stopped and waited, watchful for a trap. Sasha gave no indication that there was anything wrong. After a few minutes, he moved from cover and quietly approached Marcie. She hadn't moved and he wasn't sure she was alive.

Sasha darted ahead of him suddenly and sniffed the form on the ground. Marcie turned her head and saw the dog. She gave an ear splitting scream and tried to scramble away. Sasha jumped back, startled by the noise. She whined and looked at Dutch, ears back, looking very contrite.

"It's all right, Sasha. Marcie, are you all right?"

She turned at the sound of his voice, her face expressing disbelief firdst, then joy and relief as she recognized him. "Dutch! Oh my God, it's you! Dutch!" She started to get up but he reached her before she could and knelt beside her. She threw her arms around him and hugged him fiercely.

"Oh Dutch, thank God you came." She buried her face in his neck and began to cry in relief. The fear, with her constantly over the past hours, drained away, leaving her feeling weak and tearful.

"It's okay, Marcie, you're safe." Sasha crept forward on her belly, whining, unsure of what was happening. "Where are they? How long ago did they leave? Is Pat okay?"

Marcie was sobbing, unable to speak. He was unsure what to do besides hold her and letting her cry it out. He knew time was passing but he wasn't sure how to get Marcie to stop crying and talk to him. Finally, he held her out away from him and gave her a slight shake.

"Marcie!" His loud tone startled her and she opened her eyes. "Is Pat all right?"

She looked at him, suddenly focusing on his appearance. "Dutch, my God, what happened to your head?"

"Huh? Oh that. I got creased. Lucky shot. Is Pat okay?"

"You need to get a proper bandage on that."

"I don't have one. Now is, ..."

Trying to get up she said, "We need to get to some water and wash that. Let me take a look at it."

"Thanks Marcie, but there's no time for that right now." He brushed her hands away. "Now, is Pat okay?"

She nodded her head. "Yes. She's holding up a lot better than I am."

"How long ago did they leave?"

"I don't know, twenty minutes, half an hour."

He paused, trying to think of what to do. Meantime Sasha had reached them and was lying next to Dutch. She looked from one to the other, waiting. Dutch had made up his mind. He had to go after them now. They still had Pat and he didn't know how close they were to the helicopter. He had to get to them before they got to the chopper. He hated to leave Sasha behind but there was no other choice.

"Marcie, I'm going to leave you here and go after them." Her face instantly registered alarm. "Don't worry. I'm going to leave Sasha here with you. She won't let anything happen to you. Stay here and rest. If you feel up to it, start walking. Just follow the trail. If you don't know where it is, follow Sasha."

"Dutch please, don't leave me here by myself! I'll never find my way!"

"Yes, you will. Trust Sasha. I have to go, Marcie. I can't leave Pat with those two. You'll be fine. As soon as I find a way to let somebody know, I'll send them back for you. If not, *I'll* come back for you. I won't abandon you, Marcie." He gripped her shoulders and looked straight into her eyes. "You have to trust me, Marcie. You can do this. All right?"

She nodded numbly.

He turned to the dog. "Sasha, you stay with Marcie." He took Marcie's hand and put it on the dog's head. "Sasha, stay. You watch out for her, lead her out of here. Stay with Marcie." He took the dog's head in his hands and looked into her face. Sasha only understood the word '*Stay*' and knew she was being left in the stranger's care. Everything else he said was for Marcie's benefit.

Dutch stood up. "I'm going now. I'll be back as soon as I can or someone will be here to get you. Trust Sasha, Marcie." He looked at her for a long moment, then turned and hurried in the direction the fugitives had taken. She watched him go, fearful again, unable to say anything.

Without Marcie, their pace was initially faster. Pat tried to slow them down but Flyboy kept pulling her along. She could see that he was moving more slowly, however. He was tiring, still slowly losing blood, and his arm was obviously more painful. After struggling through some particularly tangled undergrowth, he stopped.

"Hey Mase, wait up. I gotta take a break. My arm is killing me."

"Keep movin'. We wasted too much time already. Gonna get dark soon, so keep movin'"

"I can't. I gotta rest a minute."

"Goddamn it, Flyboy, you're gonna get us caught. Suck it up and let's go!"

"Just give me a couple a minutes, Mase, just a couple a minutes." He had already slumped down next to a tree.

Mase glowered at him but could think of nothing that would get his pilot moving. Here was something else he couldn't control. He needed Flyboy. If he didn't need him to fly them out of here, he'd shoot him and leave his corpse to rot in the underbrush. *First goddamn thing I'm gonna do in Costa Rica, is learn to fly a helicopter!*

Chapter 14

"We took a look around while we were waiting for the helicopter. We found some trace in the brush where Dutch must have been waiting. We found a cell phone and a .357 along with some blood trace. Could be he was shot. What kinda pistol does he own?"

"A .357, I think. Any idea what happened?" asked Danvers.

"From the look of it, Dutch must have been shot by the fella we brought in," Simon explained.

"From the condition of the body," Roy continued, "it looks like Dutch's dog got the guy before he could finish the job. Dutch must be mobile, though. No sign he was dragged off or anything. My guess is, he patched himself up and kept going."

"Who the hell is this guy, anyway chief? I thought he just made clocks or something."

"Yeah," chimed in Roy. "He's a regular Rambo. What's his story, anyhow?"

Danvers smiled slightly. "One thing I've learned; just when you think you got folks figured out, they up and surprise the heck out of you. You two go on and get something to eat, then come back. Gonna be a long night."

The light was fading rapidly and Dutch was fighting mounting pressure. They *couldn't* be too far ahead. Marcie hadn't been much help but one of them was wounded and that would slow them down. *When it gets dark, most likely they'll stop and go to ground. If they're having this much trouble getting to the helicopter in daylight, they probably won't try moving at night.*

He looked up at the sky. It was clear, not a cloud in sight, unusual for this time of year. It meant there would be some light after sunset. He tried to remember. The moon was almost full so there would be more light come moonrise. He could rest at sunset until the moon came up, then continue on.

It wouldn't be the first time he'd travelled through wilderness at night without a night vision device. At least it wasn't swamp with the possibility of gators or cottonmouths at every step. He was hoping for a stream or creek soon. He couldn't believe they'd travelled all this way and crossed no water except for that one creek early on. *How in the hell did you manage that in the Hood?* He pushed on carefully, moving and stopping to listen often. He heard nothing, not even the silence that accompanied large creatures moving through the woods. He wasn't sure how far ahead of him they were but he needed to move faster, take a few more chances.

The sun was about to drop behind the mountains to the west and the shadows were long. They were stopped beside a small stream. Pat was washing Flyboy's wound and re-bandaging it. Blood was still seeping from the bullet holes and he seemed weaker. The fact that he might not be in shape when they did find the chopper was becoming a real possibility.

When she finished, Mase called her over. "How's he doin'?"

"Not good. He's still losing blood and infection might be setting in. I'm not sure how much longer he can go on."

"He gonna be able to fly the chopper when we get there?"

"I don't know."

"Guess."

"Then I **guess** he'll be lucky to even get to the helicopter, let alone fly it."

"Well that's too bad for him. If he can't fly, I don't need him. And if I don't need him, I don't need you."

"He needs disinfectant and antibiotics, maybe a transfusion. If I can disinfect the wound and bandage it properly so the bleeding stops, **and** pump him full of penicillin, he should be okay until you can get him to a doctor." She didn't know if any of this was true but she needed to give Mase some hope if she was going to survive.

"Well I seem to be fresh out of any of that stuff right now, so I guess Flyboy is S.O.L."

"All we need to do is get to a pharmacy. We can take what we need and you can find the helicopter and be on your way."

"Look, in case you ain't noticed lady, we're stuck in the middle of this goddamn wilderness. How are we supposed to get to a pharmacy?"

Pat's mind was racing. "We can, ... we can get to the highway and get a car, drive into Estacada. There's a pharmacy there. It's a small place and whatever police they have will be out looking for you. It won't be any problem to break in and get what we need."

"There'll be roadblocks all over. What about that?"

"They'll be looking for four men and two women, probably on foot."

Mase stood looking down at her. It could be done, and just like she said. Not for the first time he thought, *why couldn't I have someone like her in my crew, instead of these idiots?* He turned away, pacing up and down, thinking, trying to find something wrong with the plan.

"They'll get suspicious if we go into that town and come back through the same roadblock when we come back here."

"We won't need to go through the roadblock twice. There are back roads we can use to get back here without going through any roadblocks on the highway a second time."

He started pacing again, thinking. He could find nothing wrong with her plan. They could always steal a car and try for a getaway by road, but that's how most bank robbers ended up getting caught. No, the chopper was the best bet, the only sure way to get away. Much as he didn't like it, her plan was the best option.

"Okay," he said, turning to Pat, "here's what we do; first, we get to the highway. Then we stash Flyboy somewhere close to the road, and you and me go into that town and get the stuff you need. Then we get back, pick up Flyboy, get to the chopper, and split. Can we make the highway before dark?"

"I think so. This creek should be the one running out of Farley Lake. If it is, the highway should only be a mile or so from here."

"All right. Get him on his feet and let's go. I wanna get there before dark."

Sasha stopped and looked behind her. Marcie was moving slowly and carefully through the undergrowth. Her feet were suffering, her shoes almost completely disintegrated. The dog waited patiently for the woman to catch before she turned and started forward.

Marcie wasn't sure where they were going, or even if they were headed in the right direction. Every time she became worried that they might be going the wrong way, the trail became so obvious that even she could see other people had passed through. She didn't know how the dog knew where to go – by smell, she guessed.

She stopped and sat down, calling out to the dog as she did. She was tired and emotionally drained. While she was a captive, she was sure she was going to be raped or killed or both. When they left her, she was sure she was going to die of exposure or starvation. Then Dutch showed up, bloodied, like some hero in a cheap paperback.

This was a Dutch she didn't know at all. This certainly wasn't the idea spinner, the computer whiz, or the maker of clocks. This was somebody else, one of those larger-than-life types that came riding in at the last minute to save the day. *But where did all that come from? Where did Dutch get all the, . . . the what, ... skill? Was it skill? He sure didn't learn it in New York or drilling holes in wood. Who was Dutch Yancy before he was the one I knew? How did I ever let him get away?*

He found the spot by the stream where the trio had stopped. He recognized the stream. It was slightly less than a mile to the highway and the realization gave him a sinking sensation in his stomach. It probably take them less than an hour to reach it, even at a slow pace. The terrain between here and the highway was less wooded, far more open. They could make better time. He would have to do better!

He picked up his pace, jogging where he could, in spite of the pain. He slowed for a small patch of woodland, walking carefully through the underbrush and fallen branches. When he stopped and listened he could hear the sounds of the occasional passing car. Too close!

When the battered trio came in sight of the embankment, on top of which ran the highway, Mase felt a sense of relief for the first time since they'd headed into the woods. There were cars passing only occasionally, which was better than a lot of traffic. He could jack a car and have a better chance of not being seen.

There was a small stand of trees near the embankment. *Perfect spot to stash Flyboy.* The pilot was moving slower all the time and the woman was actually having to help him. She kept saying he was losing too much blood. *Well, he's gotta last a little longer. If he can get us outta here, I'll get him patched up. If he flies us outta here and then he's too far gone, at least I'm okay. I'll just hafta find another pilot.* He had them both walking ahead of him, pushing them along. It was only a hundred yards or so to the wooded patch now.

"Come on, Flyboy. Once we get to them trees, we're at the highway and you can rest. We'll grab a car and get whatever we need to patch you up, then we get to the chopper and outta here. Once we do, I'll get you to a hospital and get you stitched up properly. Hang in there, man, just hang in there."

"That was the sheriff," reported Masie. "He said they're calling off the sweeps through the Hood until daylight. They'll have more manpower available then. Meantime, the state and county will maintain the roadblocks through the night, just in case."

Her news didn't surprise Danvers. There was no sense in having people stumbling around the woods at night unless they were properly equipped and the supply of night vision devices was severely limited. The National

Guard promised some, but they wouldn't be available until the next day. Danvers hoped they wouldn't need them by then.

"Chief, why don't you go on home and get some rest?" asked Roy. "Me and Masie and Simon will split the shifts tonight and we can call you if anything happens."

"I'm gonna sleep in the spare cell tonight anyway Chief," said Simon, "so there'll be two of us handy if anything pops."

"I'll come back about two," offered Masie. "That way everybody can at least get some sleep."

Danvers looked at his three officers and felt very lucky. They were as good a crew as any small town chief could ask for. *I'm gonna hafta hammer the council about raises for this year, taxes or no taxes. If they don't come across, by God, I'll go to the voters about it!*

"Okay, but I want a call if anything, and I mean **anything**, happens. Come on, Masie, I'll give you a lift. I wanna stop by the hospital and check on Maurice anyway."

Danvers headed for the door while Roy went to the rear of the station to ensure the bed in the spare cell was made up. Simon and Masie were alone in the office for the moment.

"I'm glad you're all right. I was worried when you were out in the woods."

He walked over and took her hand. "Nothing to worry about really. I've been in more danger deer hunting. It was just a walk in the park and a nice helicopter ride."

"I know, but I was worried about what might happen."

He smiled at her. "If you want to worry, you worry about what's going to happen when I take you to dinner."

She punched his chest lightly. "Don't get overconfident, mister. I haven't agreed to go anywhere with you yet."

"But you will." He leaned down quickly and gave her a quick kiss. "That's a down payment. Now you better get out of here before the chief comes looking for you."

Chapter 15

With Flyboy safely propped against a tree, Mase headed for the highway, pushing Pat ahead of him. They climbed the bank and crossed the road. Three vehicles passed before one slowed and stopped a hundred feet or so beyond them. The driver reversed and stopped close to the pair.

He was driving an older model Chevy pickup looking somewhat the worse for wear. Pat saw it was an older man, dressed in what farmers typically wore.

He leaned over and turned the handle to lower the window. "You folks in some kinda trouble? Anything I can do ta help? Oh hey, is that you doc?" He recognized Pat.

Mase took a quick look in both directions. Nothing coming. He pulled his pistol from his belt at the small of his pack and pointed it at the man. "We need to borrow your truck for a while. Get out and walk across the road." He gestured with his weapon. "Get out. Come on," he snarled.

The man hesitated. "What the hell's goin' on, doc? Who's this bozo?"

She recognized Caleb Buckner, a farmer she had provided veterinary services to on several occasions. "Just do as he says, Caleb. I'll explain it later. Come on."

They crossed the road, descended the bank and walked into the trees. "You; s it down by that tree." He motioned at Caleb.

The old farmer hesitated, angry and confused. "Do as he says, Caleb, please," requested Pat. She was relieved when he grudgingly did as he was told.

"Tie him up, and make sure you do a good job of it. I'm gonna check when you're through."

"Tie him up with what?"

"I don't give a shit; find something. You got two minutes. If he ain't tied, I'll shoot him and save you the trouble."

Pat hesitated, momentarily at a loss; then she untucked her shirt from her jeans and reached behind her to unsnap her bra. She slipped the strap off her shoulder and down her shirt sleeve. Once it was free, she slipped it off the other shoulder and arm, then reached inside her shirt and pulled it out. She used it to tie Caleb's hands behind him and around the tree. True to his word, Mase walked over and checked the job she did. Grunting in satisfaction, he got to his feet.

"Flyboy, we'll be back as quick as we can. You keep an eye on him. If he tries to get away, shoot him." Flyboy looked tiredly at him and nodded.

"Come on. Let's get to that pharmacy and back here as soon as we can. I wanna get Flyboy fixed up and find that chopper."

Pat got to her feet and walked ahead of Mase, back to the waiting truck. She got in the driver's side and started the vehicle up. "Okay. Let's go, and don't do nothin' stupid. Drive the limit and use your head when we get to the roadblock or I'll kill you *and* the cops. You got that?" Pat nodded. As they started moving, Mase added, "I gotta hand it to ya. That was pretty slick, that thing ya done with your bra. Pretty slick." He eyed her appreciatively.

Marcie was coming to appreciate Sasha more and more. The dog stayed only a few feet ahead of her, even though she was moving very slowly. Her feet were so sore; she could only walk in spurts, depending upon the ground. When there was a clearing, fairly clear of branches and undergrowth, she could walk, hobble really, across the whole space. If it was wooded, with lots of small, sharp things on the ground, she could only go a few feet. Then she had to stop and wait until the pain subsided before she could move on again. When this happened, Sasha would come back and stand close to her until she was ready to continue. Marcie was sure the dog looked at her with a great deal of sympathy. She wondered why she had ever been worried about Sasha.

Dutch was moving quickly through the undergrowth in the fading light. As it grew darker, he had to slow down out of necessity, continuing to move as quickly as he could. He stopped and listened frequently until, in the distance, he heard the sound of a vehicle.

It's the 242; has to be. So where the hell are they? Not sure I'm still on the trail, though. Should be; looked like it was headed pretty much in a straight line, ever since they left the stream. He stepped out of the last of the trees and saw headlights passing on an elevated stretch of ground. It **was** the 242, just beyond the copse of trees ahead. *But where **are** they?*

"Say, young fella, you mind tellin' me what the hell's goin' on? Who was that guy with the doc? Who are you? How come ya got guns? Why you holdin' up folks, anyways?" Caleb Buckner was as curious as he was angry. He had yet to be afraid. "Well, come on, speak up! Least ya kin do after ya hijack my truck and kidnap me. Well, not you maybe, but that runnin' mate a yours. So, what's the story?"

"You're better off not knowing. Just take it easy. They'll be back before long and you can be on your way." Flyboy wished the old man would shut up. He was very tired and even talking was proving an effort.

"No I ain't better off. Ignorance ain't bliss, I don't care what they try ta tell ya. Only politicians believe that. Wouldn't be surprised if they was the ones thought it up. Ain't never made me happy before an' it don't now. So what was it you fellas done, anyways?"

"We robbed the bank in Sholalla."

"Damn fools," snorted Caleb. "What the hell'd ya go an' do that fer? Sholalla! They ain't got much there. You'd a been better off robbin' one over in Oregon City or Sandy maybe. Hell of a lot more money in their banks. Sholalla! What bright spark thought that one up?"

"Goddamn it, old man, just shut the fuck up!" Flyboy could feel himself getting weaker. Even raising his voice to shout at the old fart was an effort. *Why doesn't he just shut up and leave me alone? Come on, Mase, while I'm still awake.*

Dutch heard people speaking loudly somewhere ahead of him. He could still see the faint outline of a small group of trees silhouetted against the last of the fading light. That seemed to be where the sound originated. He moved as quickly and as quietly as he could toward the voices.

Pat slowed as she approached the roadblock. There were two Oregon State Police cars, their red and blue lights flashing. They were parked at angles across the lanes, forcing traffic in both directions to weave around them. She could sense Mase tensing up as she slowed to a stop and the state trooper approached the window.

"Evening, ma'am," he said, touching the brim of his blue 'Smokey Bear' hat.

"Good evening, officer. What seems to be the trouble?"

"No trouble, ma'am," he replied, looking in at Mase. "I'm just going to check the truck bed."

"Sure, go right ahead." She was surprised her voice was so calm. She felt anything but.

The policeman stepped away and in a moment he was back. "Where are you coming from?"

"Our farm, over near Whitewater. Thought we'd eat out for a change."

It seemed the officer studied her with more than passing interest. When he turned his gaze to Mase, it seemed to her that his eyes narrowed and he studied him for a long time. Finally he stepped back, touched his hat again, and said, "You folks have a nice evening now. Careful when you drive around the cars."

"Thank you, officer." Pat breathed a sigh of relief as she put the shift lever into drive and started forward. Mase remained tense until they cleared the roadblock and were entering the town limits of Estacada. "You handled that real good. Keep it up and you might survive this after all."

Dutch half crouched, moving slowly, carefully placing each foot down and testing the footing underneath before putting his weight on it. His approach was soundless. When he reached the patch of woods, he stopped. He didn't know how many people were there or who they might be. The darkness was a blessing and a curse. He waited, listening, straining to hear the rustling of leaves or branches, voices, anything. Suddenly, like the answer to a prayer, he heard a voice.

"Come on over here and loosen my hands a little. I think they're goin' ta sleep. The doc tied 'em too tight. Come on, you got the gun. I ain't gonna try nothin'.'"

Dutch crept slowly closer, toward the sound of the voice. He didn't understand what was going on but clearly, someone was tied up and someone else had a gun. *Okay; let's find the one with the gun. Wait until one of 'em speaks up again.* He hadn't long to wait.

"Ain't gonna hurt nothin' ta loosen up my hands a bit, ya know."

"For Christ sake, shut up!"

Now he knew the approximate location of both men. He moved slowly forward, toward the one with the gun.

Contrary to popular belief, when the sun goes down, you don't immediately lose your ability to see without artificial light. The moon, if it's up, gives a certain amount of illumination. A nearby town or city will give illumination, even on a cloudy night, reflecting the artificial light off the clouds. Even the stars will provide some light. Dutch was able to dimly make out two figures, propped up against trees, facing each other.

He moved quietly until he was within a couple of feet of one of the one he was sure had the gun. He carefully extended his rifle until it came in contact with the figure's head.

"Don't make a move. Don't even twitch." He spoke quietly as he crept forward and felt around for the gun. When he brushed against the man's arm, there was a grunt of pain. *Must be the pilot.* "Slow and easy does it, Flyboy. I don't want to have to shoot you again."

As he took the gun, he heard another voice say, "Who's that? Who's over there? You one a them?"

"My name's Dutch Yancy. I'm from Sholalla. Been following these guys ever since they held up the bank. Who are you?"

"Caleb Buckner. Got a farm just down the road a ways. Held me up and hijacked my truck."

"Who did?" He moved toward the other man.

"Doc Stallings and some guy I don't know. Don't reckon the doc was in on the holdup though. Seemed more like she was a hostage of the guy with her."

"She is," replied Dutch. "You got a mobile phone by any chance."

"Nope, sorry. Can't stand the damn things."

He felt the binding that had secured Buckner's hands. "What the hell is this?"

"Ain't sure myself but it looked ta me like the doc took off her bra somehow when she tied me up. Damn lucky for me, it was. That other one was threatening ta shoot me if she didn't hurry up. Quick thinker, that doc."

Dutch moved back to Flyboy and began to search him. "You got a mobile phone."

Flyboy shook his head weakly. In the almost non-existent light Dutch didn't see the movement of his head and continued to search. When he moved Flyboy's arm, he groaned.

"How's your arm?"

"Hurts. Still bleeding, I think." As far as Flyboy was concerned, it was all over, regardless of what happened when Mase returned. He knew he didn't have the strength left to fly.

Chapter 16

As they approached the drug store, Mase said, "Go to the end of the street and turn around. Park in front."

Pat's mind had been racing ever since they'd started for Estacada. She knew she was relatively safe as long as she was useful to Mase. She was useful as long as he thought she could do Flyboy some good. She was sure Flyboy had lost too much blood and was too weak now to do much of anything, let alone fly a helicopter. She didn't expect him to be conscious when they returned; she wasn't even sure he'd still be alive. At that point, her own survival would be in question.

She thought about slamming into a pole or barrier and using the airbag deployment to incapacitate Mase and give her an opportunity to escape. Since he didn't buckle up, it was a good plan. Unfortunately, Buckner's pickup was an old pre-airbag model, so that option was out. She was alert for an opportunity at the roadblock, but none presented itself.

Now they were in Estacada approaching the drug store. It was near closing time and Pat could see only a pharmacist and a female clerk in side. With Mase close behind her, they entered the store. He gripped her arm as they walked back to the pharmacy counter. At the counter, Mase rang the bell.

When the pharmacist came to the counter, Mase pointed his pistol and said in a low and quiet voice, "Call the clerk back here." When the man hesitated, Mase said in a sharper, more insistent tone, "Do it now, goddamn it, or I'll shoot her from here."

The pharmacist blanched and called out, "Sophie, can you come back here a moment please?"

The girl looked up annoyed. She was cashing out and he had disturbed her count. "All right. Coming." Pat listened to the sound of her footsteps approaching, praying that nothing would go wrong.

When the girl arrived, Mase snarled at her, "Get behind the counter with him. Both of you, keep your hands on the counter where I can see 'em." They did as they were told. The girl was terrified.

He said to Pat, "Get back and get what you need. Take him with you if you need him, but remember, any funny business and I'll kill her as quick as look at her. I know you don't want that to happen, now do you?"

"I need to ask him some questions," Pat said.

"Hurry up. I wanna be outta here in a couple a minutes."

"I've got a man with a through and through gunshot wound to the upper arm. He's lost a lot of blood. What's the best way to treat him until I can get him to a hospital?"

The pharmacist was nervous. He licked his lips and had to clear his throat before he answered. "You need to irrigate the wound with disinfectant. Keep changing the dressing and be sure to use pressure to stop the bleeding if possible. I can give you an antiseptic rinse to wash through the wound." He paused for a second. "One of the best things to use to stop the bleeding is a tampon."

"A what?"

"Depending on the size of the bullet hole, it can fit right in. It's sterile and, with the applicator, you don't have to touch it and contaminate the wound. It's an trick medics used in the Vietnam War; still do for all I know."

"Okay, let's collect what I need so we can get out of here and leave you in peace."

The man shot a nervous glance at Mase. "Okay. This way."

It only took a couple of minutes to collect a bag of supplies to treat Flyboy's wound. When Pat had what she needed, including bottled water,

Mase herded everyone to the back of the store. He found the small storage room and directed the pharmacist to unlock it. Then he took the keys from the man and pushed him and Sophie inside. He stepped in after them.

"Give me your cell phones."

"Mine's on the counter," said the pharmacist hoarsely.

Mase stared hard at him. "It goddamned well better be there when I check, or I'll be back." He turned to Sophie. "Where's yours?"

She reached into her pocket and gave him her phone with a trembling hand. Mase took the phone and turned, walking out the door. He shut the door, locked it, and pushed Pat toward the shop.

"Find the light switch."

They looked around the back of the shop and found the light panel. Mase flicked the switches and the shop was plunged into darkness. Illumination from the streetlights allowed them to make their way to the front of the store. He pushed Pat toward the door.

When they were outside, he handed her the keys. "Lock up."

She found the proper key and locked the door. Mase took the keys and dropped them, and the cell phones, into the drain at the curb. He motioned her toward the pickup and they got in. "Okay. You said there was a way back that avoided goin' through the roadblock. Go that way."

"I know you want to help, Caleb, but the best way for you to help, is to wait here with this guy until it's over. I don't want her to get hurt. I don't want a lot of lead flying all over the place if I can prevent it."

"You might be right, but by golly, I'd sure like to get a crack at that guy. Stealin' my truck really got my blood boilin'."

"Don't worry, we'll get him. Come on. I'll give you a hand moving Flyboy to the far side of the trees."

"Weird name for a guy."

"He's a pilot."

After he got Caleb and Flyboy settled, Dutch moved back to the edge of the trees. He looked around, trying to pick a spot that would give him an advantage when Mase returned. Surprise was on his side. Although the temptation to shoot first and talk later was almost overwhelming, he wasn't sure he could do that; not unless Pat was in immediate danger and it was necessary to save her.

A three-quarter moon was coming up in the northeast and the cold steely light gave some illumination. He'd given Caleb his rifle and he took Flyboy's Glock 9mm. He checked it over, ensuring there was a full magazine and a round in the chamber. *They'll be driving, using headlights. His eyes won't adjust for a while, maybe not even by the time he starts across the field to the trees. Probably best if I hit him in the field, before he gets to the trees.*

He was hoping that, whatever happened, Pat would be quick enough to get out of the way if there was any shooting. He would do everything he could to prevent it, but it all depended on Mase Krilley. He hoped Marcie was all right. Sasha would keep her safe from harm, except whatever her imagination would conjure up. He was sure she must be frightened, alone at night, in the woods, a long way from home. *Welcome to night life in Oregon!*

Marcie had gone as far as she could. Her legs were aching and her feet were too sore to put any weight on them. She sat with her back against a tree, on the verge of tears. Sasha crept forward and put her head in the woman's lap. The gesture took her completely by surprise. She put her hand on the dog's head and Sasha gave a small whine. It was as if she understood exactly how Marcie was feeling and wanted to give her support and understanding.

She'd never had a dog and never wanted one. As far as she was concerned, they were smelly, needy, unsanitary beasts that were always underfoot, slobbered all over you, barking, jumping up on you, ruining your clothes, your furniture and your life (or at least imposing in a most unwelcome manner). Sasha was different. The animal had a level of intelligence that completely surprised her. It was as if the dog understood exactly what was required and what she was supposed to do. Not only that, she seemed to know just what Marcie needed and to provide it insofar as she could. Marcie felt a wave of gratitude for Sasha's company. She wasn't sure she could survive in this wilderness without her.

"Dutch must really love you, Sasha," she said, softly stroking the dog's head. At the mention of her name, Sasha raised up slightly. "I don't know what I'd do without you here." Sasha wiggled a little closer and settled her head back down on Marcie's lap.

They passed a mile marker and Mase said, "Pull over. We're here."

Pat slowed, eased off the road onto the shoulder, and stopped. She shut off the lights and killed the engine. Grabbing the first aid supplies, she got out of the truck and hesitated. She looked across the road and then up the highway in each direction. She thought about running but the moon was providing too much light; besides, there was Caleb, tied up across from Flyboy. If she did get away, what would Mase do to him? Better to wait.

She came around the truck and descended the bank ahead of Mase. She could just make out the trees across the small field and headed directly for them. As they made their way through the grass and weeds, she thought she heard a faint rustling somewhere ahead. *Fox or rabbit maybe.*

Mase was walking a few feet behind her, splitting his attention between her and his footing. He thought he remembered the ground and being slightly irregular and he didn't want to trip and fall. It was tough to see out here and she might make a run for it. He'd have a hard time finding her without a flashlight. He cursed himself for not grabbing one from the drugstore. *I still need her to patch up Flyboy. Once we find the chopper, well, . . .* The truth was, he didn't know what he'd do with her when the time came.

The moonlight could play tricks on the eyes. There were patches of dark and light all over the field. They had just passed one dark patch when he sensed something different, almost at the same time he heard the faint sound.

"Stop where you are, Mase, and don't turn around. I want to see your hands in the air. High in the air. Now!" Dutch's voice had an ice cold, hard edge to it.

Mase froze. He didn't understand what was happening for a second. *Who the hell? What the hell? Where'd **he** come from?* He was trying to calculate where the man was, behind him or beside him, how fast and in what direction he needed to move to get a shot.

"Don't do it, Mase! I've got you cold and you know it. Don't make me shoot you. Commit suicide on your own, don't use me."

Mase stopped thinking, stopped wondering, stopped worrying. He whirled toward the sound of the voice. Pat had turned to watch and as Mase moved she dropped to the ground. Dutch was ready and, as Mase moved, he fired twice.

The first bullet caught Mase in the right shoulder and helped spin him around. He was still bringing his pistol up when the second shot hit him high in the chest on the left side, midway between his heart and his collarbone. It drove him in the other direction and he dropped his weapon as he fell toward the ground. He felt two strong pushes, driving him in opposite directions; then the pain hit him. Two searing lances of fire seemed to shoot through his upper body and he couldn't keep himself from crying out.

Dutch moved swiftly to the wounded man, now lying on his back. He knelt beside him, placing his weapon to his temple. "Keep still; don't even twitch. Pat, you okay?"

"I'm fine, Dutch. What took you so long?"

"Stopped for breakfast. You got a phone?"

"No, but he does; in his pocket."

"Come on over here and see if you can find his weapon, will you. He dropped it somewhere close and I'll feel better when I know where it is."

The vet scrambled over and Dutch could dimly see her feeling around in the grass and weeds. "Okay, I found it."

Dutch leaned back and began to search Mase's pockets. He found the phone and handed it to Pat, never taking his eyes from the wounded man.

"Call 911 and get somebody out here right away. Flyboy was looking pretty bad when I left him with Caleb. I don't know if he's going to make it, and this one's got a couple of slugs in him too. We need some light and I have to get back into the woods to find Marcie and Sasha."

She placed the call and gave the operator a quick description of the situation and directions how to find them. When she had finished, Dutch asked, "Can you go over in the trees and give a shout to Caleb, just to let him know everything is all right. I don't want him to shoot Flyboy because he's worried about what happened here."

He didn't really need Pat to do that, but he thought it best to keep her as busy as possible until the police arrived. She could fall apart then. As she moved off, he hauled Mase to his feet by the collar. He was moaning in pain and Dutch wanted to keep him moving for a few minutes until they could sit him down and start treating his wounds. They would have to do it by feel, but if they could keep him from going into shock and stop the bleeding, he might survive to see prison.

Fifteen minutes later they were all gathered under the trees. Flyboy was unconscious, his breathing shallow. Caleb had gone to his truck and brought back a flashlight so Pat could see while she bandaged Mase's wounds. There was little she felt she could do for Flyboy and she wasn't sure even the EMTs could pull him through.

Dutch watched her work on Mase and marvelled that she could bring herself to help him after what he put her through in the past ten hours. He wanted to start back for Marcie and Sasha but he would need a light and the only flashlight was needed here. Besides, he didn't want to leave Pat until the police arrived.

Pat finally got up and stepped away. "That's the best I can do for now. The bullets are still in his body but I don't think you hit anything vital. He needs to get to an ER pretty quickly, though."

Dutch stepped over to her. He reached out and put a hand on her shoulder. "You sure you're okay?"

She didn't speak immediately and he felt her shoulder start to tremble. Suddenly she fell against him and threw her arm around him. She was shaking and he could feel her start to cry. He didn't say anything, just put his arms around her and held her.

A couple of minutes later they heard the sirens and the screech of brakes as the police cars started to arrive. Caleb was waiting by his truck and over Pat's head, Dutch could see the lights of their flashlights as they slid down the bank and started across the field.

"It's okay, Pat. Police are here and they can take it from here. I think there's an ambulance too. It's all over,"

He heard her sniff and she said in a voice muffled somewhat by his shirt, "I was so scared until I heard your voice and then, I don't know, I was still scared, but not the same way. I knew you were following us and it would be all right. I was still scared that something would happen, but I knew it would be all right somwhow. Thank you."

He didn't know what to say and was saved from thinking of something as Caleb and the state troopers entered the grove of trees. There was a round of introductions and brief explanations. The paramedics arrived and began treating Flyboy and Mase. There was a brief discussion amongst the officers about who would ride with the prisoners while one officer read Mase and Flyboy their rights. One of the troopers insisted that Pat go along to the hospital for a check up. She objected that she was fine but he was insistent.

Dutch pulled one of the officers aside. "Have you got a flashlight I can borrow? There's another woman back there in the woods. She was one of the hostages they left behind and I left her back there with my dog. I'm sure she must be scared and I need to go get her and bring her out."

"Yeah sure. Do you want one of us to go along with you?"

"No, I'll be okay. I should be able to find her. If you can have a car wait here until we come back, I'd appreciate it. Don't want to have to hitchhike home."

"No problem. Someone will be here when you get back." He handed Dutch the flashlight.

"Thanks a lot." He turned to see Pat being led toward the highway and, satisfied she was being looked after, he turned and headed out across the field.

Chapter 17

While Dutch was working his way through the undergrowth trying to follow the trail back the way he'd come, Chief Corby Danvers was engaged in a lengthy conversation with the Oregon State Police. He was finishing up when his two officers returned from dinner.

"Sorry, Sid. He's a Sholalla boy and if he joins anything it'll be my department. I'm not sure he's suited to life in the fast lane with you state boys anyway." There was a pause and Danvers chuckled. "You're right about that. I'll talk to you in the morning, right after the FBI leaves. Good night."

"Hey, chief. You can go on home now. Me and Roy got this."

"We can all go home, Simon, except for whoever's staying here with the prisoner. That was the state police. They got the last two, or rather Dutch Yancy did. Pat Stallings is all right and on her way to the hospital for a check up. They recovered all the money and they're transporting the remaining suspects to the hospital."

"What about the other woman? What was her name, Marcie something?"

"Watson. She's still in the woods with Yancy's dog and he's gone in to fetch them."

"They say what happened?" asked Roy.

"They don't have all the details yet. They'll get a statement from Doc Stallings at the hospital and I'll talk to Yancy tomorrow sometime."

"I don't get it, chief. Yancy got them all; all four of them *and* rescued the hostages unharmed? Who the hell *is* this guy, Rambo Mark 2?"

"Pretty close. I had Masie pull his records. He was Marine Force Recon. He won the Navy Cross and the Silver Star on his first tour of duty in Afghanistan. Only man in the war so far to do that. He got two Bronze Stars on his second tour. He seems to make a habit of this kind of thing. His Navy Cross was for rescuing some aid workers who'd been captured by the Taliban. He went in by himself, at night, killed 17 of the enemy, and got the hostages out safe and sound. So yeah, Rambo Mark 2 is a pretty good description, except he didn't kill any of our bad guys, just put them out of action. Well, his dog finished off one, I guess."

"Damn," was all Simon could say.

"So what was that about him joining the department?" asked Roy.

"Well, I figure I could pay him half again as much as I pay you, get rid of both of you, save money, and have the lowest crime stats in the state."

The two policemen looked at each other, decidedly worried. Danvers didn't sound like he was joking.

"He's a pretty good lookin' guy and I figure Masie might be an inducement for him to join."

"Hey now, wait a minute, chief . . . . ." Simon was extremely unhappy at *that* prospect.

"Relax, Deputy Dawg. If he wanted to be in law enforcement, he would be. Besides, you two are the next best thing to Abbott and Costello and I'm used to you." He got up from his desk. "I'm going home. You two check on our guest and decide who's taking the duty to watch him. I'll see you in the morning."

It was much slower going in the dark, even with moonlight. Dutch was sure he'd lost the trail several times. When he thought he was getting close, he began to call Sasha. It was another 15 minutes before the dog heard him.

Sasha suddenly raised her head, ears up, alert. Marcie was half asleep and the movement startled her. The dog stood up, and faced away from her.

She whined, took a couple of steps away, then turned back and gave another whine and a low growl.

Marcie grew quickly alarmed. Something was disturbing Sasha and the dog was becoming agitated. She had visions of a predator coming closer; fear gripped the pit of her stomach and rose up in her throat. Sasha took a couple of dancing steps away. The dog turned and looked at her, whined, then turned and raced off into the darkness.

"Sasha! Come back! Sasha!" Marcie was terrified. She didn't know what was out there or why the dog left her. All she did know was that it was dark and getting chilly and she was alone in the woods, with no one and nothing to protect her. She pressed back against the tree and drew her knees up, circling them with her arms. She peered fearfully into the darkness and sat there scarcely breathing, for what seemed like hours.

She heard the sound of an animal moving toward her, rapidly. The sound was getting nearer. She buried her face in her drawn up knees and stopped breathing. She knew this must be the end. Suddenly there was a cold wet nose pressed against her arm and a familiar whining sound. She raised her head and felt Sasha's tongue licking her arm. She turned in the direction of the sounds in the brush and saw a moving light. She felt weak as relief flooded through her body.

"Sasha? Where are you girl? Sasha!"

Marcie had never heard anything so welcome as the sound of Dutch Yancy's voice. "Over here, Dutch! I'm over here!"

"Marcie! Hang on, I'll be there in a minute."

Suddenly he was beside her. She reached up and threw her arms around him, hugging him so fiercely she almost pulled him off balance.

He put his arms around her and hugged her for a long moment. Finally, she felt him draw back. "You okay?"

She nodded. "Just sore and scared. I didn't know what was coming through the woods." She sniffed, not even realizing she'd been crying.

"Everything is okay now. The police have the Mase and Flyboy in custody and Pat's on the way to the hospital. We need to get you out of here. Can you walk?"

"I don't think so. My feet are so sore. My shoes came apart and I'm afraid my feet are pretty cut up."

"That's okay, don't worry." He rose. "Come on, try to stand up."

She got slowly and painfully to her feet, wincing and crying out a little with the pain. He reached down and scooped her up in his arms.

"Okay, Sasha, let's go home."

Surprised, Marcie leaned her head against his neck, feeling very safe and secure for the first time since the robbery.

"Hang on. The footing might be a little tricky but we'll be out of this stuff pretty quickly."

She tightened her grip and nestled her head against him. "You take all the time you need," she murmured. An hour and a half later, two state troopers, saw a light bobbing across the field toward the grove of trees and their own lantern.

"Yancy, that you?" one of them called.

"Yo. Call the paramedics. I got one for the hospital with me."

When the ambulance arrived and Marcie was loaded aboard, Dutch asked one of the EMTs, "Can you take a look at my head and let me know if it needs attention? I got knicked and I'm not sure how bad it is. Still hurts some."

The Emergency Medical Tech peeled off the bandana and shined his light on the wound. "How long ago were you shot?"

"I don't know, a few hours I guess. I kinda lost track of time."

"I think we ought to take you in and have one of the doctors take a look. It's pretty deep and might need some stitches. Gonna leave a nasty scar, from the look of it. Go ahead, climb it with the lady."

"That's okay. I'll have one of the troopers take me in."

"Come on. We're going in anyway. No sense making them do an extra trip."

"Can't go without my dog."

"Bring him along."

He nodded and climbed into the back of the ambulance and took a seat next to Marcie, who was lying on the stretcher. She reached out and took his hand. Sasha bounded in and lay down on the floor.

"Thank you," she said. "You saved my life."

"Don't exaggerate. You would have been okay. A little cold maybe, but once they decided to let you go, someone would have found you in a few hours."

"You don't understand. That one man, Del, you didn't hear what he was saying, what he was planning to do when we got to the helicopter. If you hadn't come after us and stopped them, I'm sure they would have raped us both and then killed us. He shot that man in the bank when his hands were raised."

"Well, he won't be shooting anyone anymore."

He slumped back against the wall of the ambulance, suddenly very, very tired. The adrenaline was draining away, and he felt something he hadn't felt in a long time, something he thought he'd never feel again. He closed his eyes and a parade of images marched through his mind, places and faces from a past he thought was long behind him.

He was dozing when the ambulance stopped at the Oregon Falls Hospital in Oregon City. Dutch got out and waited while they wheeled Marcie out. He trailed after them into the ER. He waited while she was taken into one of the treatment bays, then he went to the desk and asked to see a doctor.

The nurse looked at his head and asked, "What happened?"

"Gunshot wound."

She handed him a clipboard and said, "Take a seat and fill this out. Someone will be with you as soon as possible. We're a little busy. Take that dog outside. Hospital rules don't allow animals in the building. This isn't a veterinary clinic."

He looked down at Sasha, sitting quietly at his side. He felt a sudden surge of anger. "Fuck you and your rules," he snapped. "Come on, Sasha. I'll find a vet to sew me up."

He started to walk away when one of the troopers who'd followed them in stopped him. He walked to the counter and said in a quiet voice, with an edge the nurse couldn't mistake, "He's with us, part of that robbery over in Sholalla. Treat him and we'll take care of any questions. Insurance isn't an issue here. Oh, and the dog stays. Call her a seeing eye dog, if it bothers you, but the dog stays!"

She started to object, but the look on the trooper's face changed her mind. Dutch sat tiredly in one of the chairs and had trouble staying awake. His eyes were shut so he was surprised when a voice next to him said, "Mr. Yancy; the doctor will see you now."

Pat wouldn't lie down and, after refusing for the third time to see a trauma counsellor, she was anxious to go home. Before she did, she asked about Marcie and was told she was being admitted for a few days, until she could walk. She was surprised when the nurse volunteered that Mr. Yancy would be released as soon as the doctor had finished treating him. She had just entered the waiting room, wondering how she would get home, when a state trooper approached her and asked if she would mind answering a few questions. As much as she wanted to get home and into her bed, she agreed. She asked about Dutch.

"He's getting some stitches. A bullet creased the side of his head but the doctor says it's nothing serious. Why don't we sit down over here? I only have a few questions tonight. You can give a complete statement tomorrow or the next day."

His few questions stretched into an hour and when he had finished, Pat could hardly stay awake. The trooper asked her to wait for a moment while he arranged for transportation. She was staring at the wall, not seeing anything really, when she realised there was someone standing next to her. It was Dutch, and Sasha was pushing against her leg.

"Oh Dutch. I'm sorry, I didn't see you there. Are you all right? The policeman said you'd been shot." She ran her hands over the dog's neck and shoulders. "Hello, Sasha, how are you?"

He sat down heavily next to her and leaned back in the chair. "Just a crease, nothing serious. How you doin'?"

"I'm fine. Nothing worse than I'd get from a walk in the woods on Sunday."

"Some walk."

"Listen, Dutch, I . . . well, I don't even know how to thank you and Sasha for what you did. That was a big chance you took, coming after us like that, but if you hadn't, well . ."

"It's okay, Pat, you don't have to thank me," he cut her short. "After all, I have money in that bank and I couldn't let them walk off with it, now could I? A biscuit for Sasha would be nice though." He gave her a tired smile. The dog looked from one to the other, as her name was mentioned.

For some reason, his response irritated her. "It isn't a laughing matter, Dutch. You could have been hurt; killed."

"Coulda, woulda, shoulda. I wasn't killed, *or* hurt; okay, hurt a little, maybe. What do you expect me to do, curl up in a ball, sucking my thumb while I wait for the shrink?" he snapped. "You can stand and watch or you can act; I acted. Call it conditioned response, Pavlov's dogs, whatever." His tone softened. "Sorry, I get a little cranky when I'm tired. Anyway, it doesn't matter. It's over and right now I'm just too tired and sore to argue with you, doc." He leaned back in the seat, placed his head against the wall, and closed his eyes. He felt her hand gently touch the bandage around his head.

"You're right about the *hurt* part. Looks like part of you didn't dodge the bullet."

"Cute, Stallings, real cute. It's only my head, doc; no harm, no foul."

She watched as his features gradually relaxed. He would be asleep in a minute and she hoped that their ride would be here soon so she wouldn't have to wake him. As if reading her thoughts, he said, "Just resting my eyes. Nudge me when our ride is here."

Late the next afternoon, Dutch went into the police station to give his statement. He tried to keep it brief, factual and simple. He was continually interrupted by either Simon or Roy with requests for embellishment on some point or other, or questions about why he did something. After an hour and a half, he'd had about enough.

"Look guys, I'm not here running some kind of tactical post mortem. I want to wrap this up. The last part is pretty simple. I waited in the field and when Mase came back with Pat Stallings, I was behind him and got the drop on him. I told him to drop his gun. He decided to try it and I shot him twice, once in the shoulder and once in the chest. I stuck around while Pat patched him up. When the state troopers showed up, I went back in the woods and found Marcie Watson and Sasha. She couldn't walk so I carried her out. We got in the ambulance and went to the ER.

"That's about all there is to it. If you have any more questions about what happened, let me know. Meantime, I've wasted about enough time on bank robberies and bank robbers. They ran, I caught 'em, the rest is up to you and the courts. Now, if there's nothing else, I need to get up to the hospital."

Roy started to ask another question when Simon interrupted him. "That should do it, Mr. Yancy. Thanks a lot. I don't think you'll have to testify. It's a pretty open and shut case." He paused. "Oh, before you go, the chief asked me to have you sign this form."

Dutch took the paper and scanned it. "What's this?"

"It's the form that signs up as a reserve deputy, backdated six months."

"What's this for?"

"Chief's worried that some smart ass lawyer might get those three off on some technicality since you were in pursuit and not technically a law enforcement officer. This way you have been a member of the Sholalla Police Department for the past six months and as such, duly authorised to pursue and apprehend anyone breaking the law."

Dutch frowned, thought about it for a minute, then signed. "There an initiation ceremony or anything?" Simon shook his head and grinned. "Okay. See ya." With that, he left the station and almost ran into Pat Stallings on his way out.

"Oops, sorry Pat. How are you?"

"I'm fine. A good night's sleep was just what I needed. How's your head?"

Unconsciously his hand went up to the bandage wrapped around his head. "Still a little sore. I'm not sure why they thought they had to wrap me up like an Arab sheik, though."

"I don't know; it's sort of becoming."

"Next you're going to tell me about some bargain swampland you got for sale in Florida."

She grinned, then her expression turned serious. "Listen, Dutch, I never did get to. . ."

He looked pointedly at his watch and interrupted her, "Sorry Pat, but I have to go. I'm going to miss visiting hours at the hospital if I don't hurry."

"Marcie?"

He nodded. "She should be on the mend and headed back to New York soon."

"Did she tell you why she came to see you?"

"No. Did she say anything to you?" Pat shook her head. "I'll have to ask her. Say, you should stop by and see her too. She's probably kinda lonesome."

"Maybe I will."

"Okay. See ya."

"See you, Dutch."

Marcie was sitting up in bed when Dutch walked into her room. Her face lit up when she saw him. "Dutch! It's so good to see you!"

"Hi Marcie. How are you feeling?"

"Lots better. My legs still ache and my feet are sore, but it's nothing serious. The doctor says I can go home tomorrow or the next day. There's no permanent damage. I'll have to take it easy for a while and it may be uncomfortable walking for a week or so."

"That's good. Wouldn't want you taking home any horrible lasting souvenirs of your visit. Talk to Arthur?"

"Yes. He was very sweet and told me to take as long as I needed to recuperate."

"Thoughtful of him."

"Maybe, but I bet he has interviews lined up with some of the trade journals. You know, *'Teasdale Partner Kidnapped By Bank Robbers'*, *'Watson Survives Oregon Ordeal'*, that sort thing. Good publicity for the firm and all."

"Tough way to get it."

She nodded. "Yes it was." She paused. "Dutch, I want to say thank you again. I don't know why you did what you did, but I'm so, so grateful you came after us. I told you, and I told the police; you saved my life. Pat's too."

"What's important is that everything was all right in the end and you're okay. Besides which, you have one hell of a story to tell on the cocktail party circuit." He smiled at her.

"Where did you learn to do all those things? Not in New York at Teasdale's."

"I was in the Marines a while back. They gave us some pretty good training and I guess some of it stuck."

"I heard some of the police talking. They were saying something about medals you won in Afghanistan. Is that true?"

He shrugged. "Victim of circumstance."

"You're just being modest. They were very impressed, the way they talked."

"It sounds a lot more impressive than it really was. Anyway, you'll be headed back to New York then, in a couple of days."

"I guess. Before I go, I'd like to talk to you. There's a wonderful opportunity that's come up and I think you should consider it."

"We can talk now."

"I'd rather wait until they release me. Can you come get me when they do? We can go to dinner, my treat."

"Sure. I never say no to Teasdale's expense account."

"Okay. I'll call you. I'd like to see Sasha too. I understand why you like dogs now."

"She's more than just a dog."

"Yes, I know."

"I'm going to go, let you get some rest. Call when they're going to spring you and I'll pick you up. By the way, the chief says they won't ticket your car, even though you are illegally parked."

She smiled. "Oregon hospitality?"

"We're a very friendly state."

Chapter 18

Pat was having coffee with Masie Alcott. She'd met Masie when she first came to Sholalla and the police officer and the vet had been friends ever since. Pat was a very private person, but Masie Alcott was the one person she confided in. It was two days after the robbery and things were returning to normal. Pat had finished her office hours and met up with Masie for the first time since her ordeal.

"How are you doing?" asked Masie. "Things getting back to some semblance of normality?"

Pat nodded. "Slowly."

"Something like what you've been through can be hard to shake off. Any after effects?"

"You mean nightmares, the shakes, stuff like that?" Masie nodded. "No, not really. It's just trying to get to grips with the fact that there are actually people out there like Mase Krilley and Del Ross and they're real, not characters on a TV show."

"I know. It's hard even for me to believe somebody would rob our bank. Makes you think no place is safe anymore."

"Probably true."

"Have you talked to Dutch since?" Masie knew about their date and the kiss.

"We bumped into each other at the station, but he was in a hurry to get to the hospital to see Marcie so we didn't really have a chance to talk."

"What about this Marcie, anyway? You think there's anything going on between them?"

Pat shrugged. "I don't know. She sounded like she just stopped in for a visit but . . . ."

"But?"

"From what she told me in the woods, she had something important to talk to him about. There was something going on between them back in New York evidently."

"Did she say what kind of something?"

"Not exactly. I got the impression that Dutch was into her but she just couldn't see it or him as anything but a work relationship."

"So they were in the Friend Zone."

Pat nodded. "She sounded like she might be out here to correct her oversight."

"He's something else, that Dutch Yancy. Did he ever say anything about being in the service?"

She shook her head. "I figured he might have been, the way he handled himself out there in the Hood, but he never talked about it. Why? What did you find out?"

"When the chief found out he was trailing you, he had me check. He was Marine Corps Force Recon; served two tours in Afghanistan in the early years. He won the Navy Cross and a whole slew of other medals. That boy is a genuine, dyed in the wool, red, white and blue hero and about as tough as they come. He's the real deal."

Pat didn't respond immediately. She thought for a moment. "He could have killed Mase out there in that field, without giving him a chance. I think he would have been justified, but he didn't. He gave him a chance to surrender and even when Mase turned to shoot him, he still only wounded him. I think it takes a lot to practice restraint like that."

"Okay, now that everybody agrees Dutch Yancy is all man and a yard wide, what are you going to do about it? When word gets around about him, every single gal in the county is gonna be lining up at his door to do more than buy a clock."

"I don't know, Masie. I think he's still carrying some kind of torch for Marcie. Now that she's here, I think it may be too late."

"Never too late to go after what you want. From what you said about that kiss he gave you, I think he had more than just a match lit for you. At least he did before you blew him off. You need to tell him, you know."

"Tell him?"

Masie nodded. "Everything."

"What if he doesn't understand?"

"Then he's not the right guy for you, is he?"

"It may be too late," Pat repeated.

"You won't know 'til you try."

Dutch looked across the table at Marcie. He thought she looked as attractive now as she did three years ago. Maybe it was a trick of the light. The restaurant in Portland seemed to depend more on candlelight than electric lamps. The cynic in him said it was probably to disguise the overpriced entrees but it did seem to have an enhancing effect in Marcie's appearance.

She was dressed in a black dress that clung in all the appropriate places. She wore slippers and walked slowly and gingerly on feet that were still sore, but at least she could move around and drive a car.

She's going all out tonight; champagne, lobster, the works. He appreciated the gesture but had the feeling there was more going on than just dinner. He'd seen her wine and dine prospects any number of times. *What I did was as much about Pat as it was her.* He'd like to believe he would have gone after Mase and his bunch even if they didn't have hostages, but down deep he suspected he probably would have left it up to law enforcement. Pat and Marcie were the reason he did what he did. *If it was just Marcie or just Pat, would I have done it?* He knew he would have.

"You know, it's very rare when someone actually steps in and saves you; I mean literally saves you, like in the movies. It's rarer when you get a chance to thank them, so thank you, Dutch. You are now officially my hero." Marcie raised her glass in a toast.

Dutch smiled at her. "And it's common for people who happen to be in a position to do something in a situation like that, to be embarrassed about it afterwards when people make a fuss. It's also common for them to be more embarrassed when someone calls them a hero. Believe me, Marcie, I am **not** a hero."

"Well you are to me."

"Okay, but do me a favour now, and drop all this hero stuff. It really is embarrassing."

"As you wish – hero." She gave him a wicked grin.

They finished their meal and were having after dinner drinks when Marcie suddenly said, "Dutch, I want to talk to you about something serious."

"Sure. What's on your mind?"

"You are."

"You aren't going to start that hero business again, are you?"

"No, this is about something else. It's about your clocks, the wood ones, the ones you make out of,.. whatever that stuff is."

"Burls," he furnished.

"Burls. I spoke to Arthur while I was in Seattle. A client was in the office and saw the clock you gave me. He got really excited and wants to talk about contracting you to provide his company with a number of them. They are the largest provider of top quality room décor in the Northwest. The initial order he's talking about will be worth six figures. This could be something amazing for you Dutch."

What she said took him totally by surprise. He had never considered large scale production of his clocks before, at least not the burl clocks. He didn't even see how it was possible. "How many clocks was he talking about?" he asked.

"I'm not sure. From what Arthur said, at least a thousand."

"A thousand!" In the three years he'd been here he'd only made a hundred or so. How long would it take to make a thousand, provided he could find enough burls? "I don't see how I could do that. It would take years for me to make that many. The shipping costs alone would be substantial."

"I'm sure there are things you could do. You could relocate to New York, for starters. That would take care of the shipping costs."

"Relocate? Why would I relocate?" He liked it here. He didn't want to live anywhere but where he was now.

"To be close to your customer. They have trees in New York you know, thousands of them. You wouldn't have to make the clocks yourself. You could train people to do what you do. You'd be providing employment and opportunity to a lot of people who have artistic talent, who can see the same beauty in wood that you do. It's only the start. You could introduce people all over the country to burl clocks; all over the world, possibly."

It was obvious that she had given this some serious thought. Something on this scale never occurred to him. "I don't know, Marcie. I never considered anything like this. I'm not sure I want to be involved in an operation on that scale. I make clocks because I like to make clocks. I like creating something beautiful from a piece of nature that would otherwise go to waste. Ramping it up to a commercial operation, well . . . I'm not sure. I'll have to think about that."

"Why don't you come back to New York with me and meet with the client; at least hear what he has to say and understand exactly what it is he's after? Get it from him first hand and then make up your mind. It'll only take a couple of days. If you don't like what you hear, you can walk away."

By God, she's good, you have to give her that. Do I want to go to New York; certainly not the city, upstate maybe. There's always lots of other places, I suppose; Maine, Vermont, New Hampshire. Lots of trees and plenty of small towns like Sholalla.

"I don't know, Marcie. I have to give this some thought."

"Look, I'm going back day after tomorrow. Why don't you sleep on it and let me know by late tomorrow what you decide. Remember, this isn't a commitment of any kind, just an exploratory meeting."

He nodded. "All right. I'll call you tomorrow."

"There's something else I want to talk to you about, but it can wait until tomorrow."

"Fair enough. We'll talk tomorrow."

He had a pretty restless night and didn't accomplish much the next day. He thought about the offer Marcie made and what it could mean; what it would mean. There was a lot to gain. The money would be nice. Expansion would mean his name, his creations, would be seen by many more people. He would be making his mark. National and even international markets were a distinct possibility.

But there would also be things to lose. The clocks were his expressions, his creative vision. Expansion would mean they would be the expression of other people's creative vision. It would mean leaving Sholalla, the people, Leroy and LeeAnn and the kids. He would still have Sasha but he would also be uprooting her; and he would be leaving Pat Stallings. Much as he believed the idea of anything romantic with the vet was over, he didn't like the idea of not seeing her again.

He still needed to talk to her, to find out why she had been so reluctant to agree to another date. *Should I make a decision before I have a chance to speak to her? Would it hurt to at just go to New York and talk? I won't be agreeing to anything, just listening.*

He was relatively sure he wouldn't go for a large scale deal, but maybe there was a possibility that he could work out something on a smaller scale. A ready market for his clocks would be a welcome change and provide a level of security he'd never had since he started making clocks. *Okay, why not go and see what the man had to say?*

He was about to call her when Pat Stallings suddenly came through the front door of the workshop with Sasha trailing after her. "Hello, Dutch. Just thought I'd stop by on my way to Caleb Buckners."

"How's he doin'? He over his 'mad' yet, about getting his truck hijacked?"

She smiled. "Not yet; maybe by Christmas."

She started to say something else when he said, "I'm glad you came by; need to ask you for a favor. You want some coffee?"

"Sure. What's up?"

He waited until she was seated before he asked her. "I was wondering if you could take care of Sasha for two or three days? I have to go out of town and I can't take her with me."

"Sure, anytime, you know that. Where are you headed?"

"New York."

She felt her guts twist into a knot. "Oh. Marcie?"

Was that a hint of disappointment in her voice? "In a manner of speaking. She has a client, or rather her firm does, and apparently he likes my clocks and wants to discuss buying a quantity. I thought I go and see what he has to say; see what kind of deal he's offering."

"It sounds promising."

"Mmmm, maybe."

"You don't sound so sure."

"It would mean relocating to New York or New England someplace, and I don't know if I want to do that. I could, easy enough; nothing tying me here really. I just don't know. I guess I'll see what the guy has to say and make up my mind then."

She needed to leave, and right now. She didn't want to sit across from him and listen to him talk about leaving. She couldn't. She looked at her watch. "I better be going. What time will you be dropping Sasha off?"

"Is it all right if a call you when I know what the travel arrangements are?"

"Sure; that will be fine. Thanks for the coffee. Talk to you later, Dutch."

"Okay Pat, thanks."

She drove away but had to stop a half mile down the road. The tears in her eyes made it difficult to see and too dangerous to drive.

On the flight to New York, Dutch was in coach, or cattle class as he called it, while Marcie was up front in First Class. She wanted to pay for the ticket but he insisted on covering his own expenses. He didn't want to feel obligated to anyone for any part of this trip.

He'd met Marcie at the airport and she was getting about better. Her feet were still sore but seemed to be healing fast. They were busy with security and check in and didn't really have much chance to talk before they boarded the plane.

Once they were airborne, Marcie asked if Dutch could come up to first class. There was an empty seat next to her and the cabin supervisor agreed. Marcie also talked them into an extra champagne glass for him.

"Cheers," toasted Marcie, holding up her glass.

"Here's mud in your eye," replied Dutch, touching his glass to hers.

"Quaint."

"You know what they say; you can take the boy out of Oregon. . ."

"You'd think you were native born or something."

"Feels like it sometimes. Something in the air, I reckon."

After another glass of champagne, Dutch did what he always did in an airplane – he went to sleep. Even when he was in the Marines, if it was a long flight they would have to wake him just before a parachute jump!

Marcie would have liked to talk with him, to broach the subject of their relationship, or non-relationship or possible relationship, but was content in the knowledge that he would be in town for at least two days and she would have plenty of time to talk to him in a far more conducive atmosphere than an airplane at 35,000 feet.

She woke him before landing so he could return to his seat. When they landed, Dutch saw her safely into a taxi while took another cab to his hotel. He agreed to meet her at the office later. She offered him accommodation at her apartment but he gave her a strange look and declined. She wondered if she might have pushed a little too much.

Dutch arrived at Teasdale's before Marcie and made his way to Arthur Teasdale's office. He tapped lightly at the door and was greeted by a smiling faced Teasdale.

"Dutch m'boy, come in, come in. What are you doing knocking? No one else around here does." He took Dutch's proffered hand in both of his and shook it warmly. "How are you? You are looking marvellously well. Didn't get *that* tan in a salon, did you?"

"Hello Arthur. You're looking very well yourself. I think you look younger than you did when I left. My departure have anything to do with that?"

"Quite the opposite. Come in, sit down. Can I get you a drink? Jack Daniels if I remember correctly."

When they were settled with their drinks Teasdale said, "I understand you're the reason Marcie was able to return safe and sound. That was quite a heroic feat, Dutch. I'm grateful."

"Don't make too much of it, Arthur. The police would probably have nailed them before anything bad would have happened to her. I just happened to be at the right place at the right time."

"That isn't the way I hear it, Dutch. Your modesty does you credit. As I understand, your exploits have all the makings of a Bruce Willis movie. Well done, m'boy, well done. On another subject, what do you think of the offer our client is making? Could be very big."

"I don't know until I get some details. It's nice to have your work appreciated, of course, but it may be too big. I'll see what's on the table and think about it."

"Obviously you like where you are now or you wouldn't have been there this long. Marcie mentioned something about you having a wolf dog. Is that true?"

"Absolutely. Greatest thing on four legs. After her little adventure, even Marcie's a fan, and that's high praise from a non-dog person."

As if on cue a voice came from the doorway, "Did I hear my name being bandied about?" and Marcie swung in on her crutches.

The men both stood. Teasdale looked concerned when he saw her crutches. "Are you all right my dear? I didn't realize you were hurt so badly."

"It's nothing that a couple of weeks off my feet won't cure, Arthur. I will warn you; if you're going to visit Dutch, wear hiking boots, just in case."

"Come in, come in. Sit down and let me get you a drink."

"Just a very small one please. Dutch and I have a dinner appoint with Ellsworth Jacoby to discuss his offer. Should prove a very exciting evening."

"Careful Marcie," cautioned Dutch, "eggs and chickens."

"I really blew it, Masie. I don't think he's coming back, at least not to stay." Pat sat with Masie in a back booth and The Watering Hole Bar, nursing a Vodka Collins while Masie sipped a Coors Light. "She's got him in New York and he's going to get this really great offer. The last we'll see of him is when he comes back to pack up and move."

"You don't *know* that, Pat. Didn't you say he had reservations?"

"Probably not very big ones; at least they didn't seem very big when he was talking about it. He's back there and he lived and worked there for years before he came here. He's familiar with the place, probably has a lot of friends there, and if this guy offers him a pot load of money, why wouldn't he go?"

"Well remember, New York isn't here; it isn't Oregon. He left there to move here and he settled in once he got here. He may not want to give it all up."

"But **she's** there and you can bet she'll be working on him the whole time he's there. She let a good thing get away because she wasn't paying attention. She won't make that mistake again. She wants him and she's going to try to get him. Besides, he doesn't think there's anything to keep him here."

"He doesn't really believe that."

"He said so; exact words. My own stupid fault. I blew it."

"If you love him, fight for him, Pat. And don't give me that look. I think you do love him or you're darned close to it. It's not like you to give up."

"Great idea but, in case you haven't noticed, we're in Oregon and he's in New York."

"You'll think of something. I have faith in you."

The insistent ringing of the phone woke him and he fumbled for the receiver. "Mmmm," was all he could manage.

"Dutch? Is that you? It's Marcie. Are you up?"

"Mmmm."

"You don't sound so good."

"Mmmmm."

"Grab a shower and I'll be there in 45 minutes. We can talk over breakfast."

"You are a sadist, woman." He hung up the receiver. Downstairs 50 minutes later, he was seated across the dining room from her, nursing his second cup of coffee.

"Feeling better?"

"Marginally. My tongue's asleep and my teeth itch and I have a headache in my left eye, but other than that, I'm just peachy."

"My God, Dutch, it wasn't *that* late and we didn't drink *that* much."

"Speak for yourself, Watson."

"What did you think of Jacoby's offer?"

"Very generous."

"And?"

"And what?"

"Are you going to accept?"

"I don't know. I have to think about it."

"What's to think about? He's offering to make you rich and put your creations in some of the wealthiest and most beautiful homes in the country. You'll be famous in no time."

"Like I said, I'll think about it." He paused to drink some of his coffee. "You're pushing this awfully hard, Marcie. What you're interest in all this."

She was quiet for a few moments, considering her response. He was content to wait. Finally she said, "You."

Her reply surprised him. "Me?"

She nodded. "I was talking to Pat about something, when we were in the woods, and I started thinking. I've been doing a lot of thinking since, mostly about you and me."

"You and me? As I recall, there never *was* a you and me, was there? Did I miss something?"

"No and yes. When you were here before, I was so wrapped up in me and what I was doing, I didn't really see anything else; or *anybody* else, for that matter. Actually, I was a selfish piece of work. I didn't see you right there in front of me. Pat asked me what we used to talk about. When

I thought about it and remembered, you always listened and you somehow always made it about me. The thing was, I *let* you do it. I was so wrapped up in me, I didn't see you there too. I'm sorry about that. That apology is long overdue."

"It's ancient history, Marcie. That was then, this is now. The past is just that - past."

"I know we can't change it. That's all history, but it's *our* history, and maybe there's a chance we can pick whatever was good out of it and build on that. I guess what I'm asking you, is there a chance we could start over and try for a different outcome."

He started to answer but she continued hurriedly. "I don't mean do the same thing over and hope for a different outcome. I mean start again with me paying attention this time. I see you, Dutch. I know who you are. I can see the man I didn't even know existed and I want to know more. People change. When things like that happen, it changes you. I think we could be something special, if you want to try again. What do you say?"

When she started talking he had a feeling he knew where this was going. He should have stopped her before she said all these things, but he didn't. Now that it was out there, he had to deal with it and do something he really didn't want to do.

"Marcie, I appreciate everything you said. At first I was inclined to think this is emotional hangover from your experience, but I realise it's not. If we were the old Dutch and the old Marcie, maybe we could; maybe we could start over, or anew, whatever. Even if we were the new Marcie and the old Dutch we probably could. But I'm not that guy any more. You're still New York, Sex and the City; I'm Oregon, more Longmire I guess.

"We had our innings Marcie, and I have some good memories about those years, but there's no do-over here. A part of me will always love you, but as someone from my past." When he finished she saw the hint of a small sad smile on his lips.

Neither one said anything for a time. Marcie tried to push back a wave of sadness that washed over her, and she felt the tears start to form. She knew that it could end like this, but she hoped it wouldn't. She had to give it a shot. Now it really was over, with no chance to breathe life back into the corpse of a romance that never was.

"You're not going to take the deal."

"Probably not. I like my life, Marcie. I don't want to be big. I don't want to oversee other people do what I love to do. I'll sell Ellsworth clocks, but ones that I make in the numbers I make 'em. That's the best I can do and all that I'm prepared to do."

"It's Pat, isn't it?" she asked finally.

"What's Pat?"

"She's the one you want."

He slowly shook his head and she thought he looked a little sad. "Once maybe, but she made it pretty clear that she's not interested, so no, it's not Pat. It's not anybody."

"I'm sorry, Dutch. I didn't mean to put you in the spot. I just had to find out. That's actually what I originally intended to come see you for, before the Ellsworth offer. Now I know. It's my own fault, really. At least now I don't have to wonder anymore." She paused and looked at him. "Are you going back?"

"As soon as I can book a flight."

She nodded. "A word of advice?"

"Sure. I'm always open to advice from old friends."

"I wouldn't give up on Pat just yet if I were you." He started to object but she continued. "She always had faith that you would come for us. As soon as she saw your van she knew you were following us and it would only be a matter of time before you rescued us. She knows how special you are, Dutch, unlike me, at least like I used to be. Don't write her off just yet. Give her a chance."

"I don't know, Marcie."

"I do." She stood and Dutch got up and stood in front of her. "You take care of yourself."

She gave him a little smile. "Don't worry about me, Dutchman; I always land on my feet. I'll just have to be careful that I land lightly for a while."

She put her hand up to his face and looked into his eyes for a moment. "You'll always be the one I let get away, Dutch, and I think I'll always regret it." She kissed him lightly on the lips, then turned and made her way slowly out of the restaurant.

Chapter 19

It was two weeks since the bank robbery and it was still the main topic of conversation in Sholalla. Of course, you couldn't talk about the robbery without talking about the exploits of Dutch Yancy and his dog, with Pat Stallings and the recuperation of Maurice Chambers a somewhat distant second. Dutch was back and he tried to resume his normal routine but he found that his standing in the community had altered radically. Whenever he went into town and wherever he went in town, people stopped to engage him in conversation, sometimes for no other reason than to enquire about his health. He found this not only disconcerting, it was downright annoying.

Chief Danvers, State Police officers, *and* the FBI had stopped by his place to take additional statements. The one person who **didn't** stop by was Pat Stallings. He found this puzzling.

When he stopped to pick up Sasha, she was on her way out to an appointment and didn't have time to talk. With all that had happened he thought she would have stopped by and he would have a chance to talk about where they could go from here. Apparently, the next time he saw her would be eight months from now, when Sasha was due for her shots.

With all the interruptions and conversational delays he'd been having, he was finding it difficult to get any work done, and the orders were starting to pile up. *Maybe I need to take another break and go to LeRoy's for a few days. I'm damn sure not getting much done around here.*

"What do you think, Sasha? You want to spend some time with the kids?" Sasha sat up and cocked her head, ears erect. "I'll take that as a yes, then."

He was about to call and arrange for his visit, when he heard a vehicle in the driveway. When he looked out, he was surprised to see Pat's truck. *Well, well, will wonders never cease?*

She stopped halfway to the door, Sasha dancing around in front of her. She knelt down and rubbed her hands over the animal. *Takin' a long time with Sasha.* When she finally finished with the dog, Pat got up and walked into the shop.

"Mornin' doc. Coffee?"

She nodded. "Yes, please." She trailed him back to his living quarters, with Sasha a respectful distance behind.

When they were seated at the table with their cups, Dutch said, "I'm not going to ask you how you're doing. You must be sick of hearing that by now."

She smiled in agreement. "And I'm sure you're sick of being compared to John Wayne, Rambo and Mark Wahlberg."

"Mark who?"

"You don't watch television, go to movies?"

"Guilty."

They drank their coffee in silence for a few moments and it was not a comfortable silence. Something was badly out of whack and it was obvious to both of them.

"Look, Pat, you may think this is okay, and maybe you don't want to talk about it, but I do. I'm not a beat-around-the-bush kinda guy, so why don't you tell me what's going on."

She looked slightly exasperated. "Oh for god's sake, Dutch, I'm **sick** of talking about it, and so should you be, or maybe you like all this adulation. Besides, you're not going to be around much longer anyway. In fact, I'm surprised you're still here now." There was an angry edge to her voice that he didn't understand at all

"Adulation? What the hell are you talking about? And why the hell shouldn't I be here – I *live* here!" He was confused.

"What are *you* talking about?" Now *she* was confused.

"Some unfinished business we have."

"It doesn't matter. You're moving to New York."

"Really? When did this news break?"

"I knew what would happen when you left with Marcie. She's in love with you, or she wants to be, but you know that. With her and that big money offer, of course you're moving. You'd be crazy not to."

He gave her a small grin. "You wouldn't be the first person to say that."

"You're not . . .?"

"I'm not."

"Oh," was all she could manage.

"Now, about our unfinished business, . . ."

"You mean, . . ."

"That's exactly what I mean. Look, Pat, I thought we had a pretty good time that night. I thought so right up to and including the minute I turned and walked to my car at your house. Then, the next day it was like it never happened, or at least, not the date I remembered. Did I screw up somewhere? If I did fine, but I would like to know what it was exactly that went wrong."

"No, Dutch, it was nothing you did. It was a wonderful evening. It had nothing to do with the date or you at all."

"Well then? And please, for Christ's sake, *do not* say 'it's not you, it's me'; please. That's the oldest dodge in the world when you don't want to tell what's really going on."

She paused and looked down at the table. When she looked up, she met his gaze and said, "In this case, it happens to be true." Before he could respond she continued, "There's so much about me that you don't know."

"Are you kidding? I know almost nothing about you. So tell me why it's you and not me."

She paused and looked away, unsure if she really wanted to do this. When she turned back and looked at him for a long moment, she knew she had to.

"Back in high school, I fell for a boy in the class above me. I was a sophomore and he was a junior. I was sure it was the real thing, like you do when you're 15 and sure you'll just die if you don't see him every day. He was a really nice sweet boy and one night we were out driving and he'd been drinking, but I didn't know it. When I realised it, I told him to take me home, but he wouldn't. We were arguing about it and he wasn't paying attention to the road. He ran up over the curb and into a bus stop. We killed a 17 year old girl and her mother.

"After that I didn't trust myself to date anybody for a long time; until I was ready to go to college, in fact. Just before I left for college, I met a soldier. He was young, like me, and just out of basic training. We fell in love and we planned to get married when he got discharged. He went to Iraq and when he came back, he'd changed. He was quieter and sort of withdrawn. I shrugged it off. He still loved me and that was all that mattered.

"He went on a second tour and when he returned, he had really changed. He was moody, bad tempered, withdrawn, and he seemed angry at everyone and everything. He came to see me at school and we went out for drinks. One of the boys in my class came over to speak to us and we chatted for a minute. Derek just lost it. I don't know if he thought the boy was making a pass at me or something was going on between us or what. He jumped up and started beating the boy up. Someone called the police and when they got there, the boy was unconscious and a bloody mess. The police tried to arrest Derek and he put up a fight. In the struggle to subdue him, one of the policemen got him in a choke hold and he died as a result of the injuries he suffered." She paused.

"I'm sorry about that, Pat. It happens. Some guys should never be sent back. It isn't the combat, it's what comes after it, as a result of what you've seen and done. Sometimes you need help and hopefully you're smart enough to admit it. None of this was your fault, you know."

"Maybe. It put me off men for the rest of my time in college. When I got out and just started as a junior trainee at a big practice, one of our clients started to pester me to go out with him. He was wealthy, well groomed, and very nice, impeccable manners. The other girls thought I was crazy for putting him off. The more I put him off, the harder he tried until he finally wore me down. We had a wonderful time. He took me to all the most expensive places and gave me some really extravagant gifts. One night, coming out of a restaurant, we were arrested by DEA agents and booked. It took them a week to decide I really didn't know anything about his drug dealing and wasn't involved in any of the killings he ordered. I gave back all of the expensive presents and swore off men for good."

"Why? Nothing that happened was your fault."

"In a way it really was. I wouldn't have been caught up in any of it except for my terrible choices in men. I picked them, each one, and each one had serious faults or problems. I just couldn't see any of them. I have terrible taste in men, Dutch. I just can't trust myself when it comes to picking men."

"Yet you went to dinner with me, after you swore off men."

She didn't answer, just sighed and looked down at the table.

"Come on, Pat, why me? Why did you go to dinner with me? You could have refused."

"I know. To be honest, Dutch, I don't know why I said yes. I didn't even think about it. I was going to call and cancel, and then I found myself starting to look forward to it."

"So what's the problem? It was dinner and a kiss. Quite a kiss, I grant you. Jarred me down to my bootstraps and raised my blood pressure to an ungodly level, but it wasn't a lifelong commitment. You think another date would be the kiss of death?"

"No, of course not. It's just that, . . . well, ..."

"Just what? I might be like all the others, fatally flawed or destined for an untimely demise. Hell Pat, after what we survived, do you really believe that?"

"No, I, . . . I don't."

"We've known each other how long? Do you think I'm unstable or have some unscrupulously bad habits?"

She looked up and grinned. "***Unscrupulously*** bad habits?"

"Best I could do on the spur of the moment. I'm not good, extemporaneously speaking."

She giggled. "I think you have a terrible habit of using some atrocious words - atrociously."

"Pots and kettles, Stallings."

Her smile faded and she looked at him with a very serious expression. "To answer your question no, I don't think you're unstable or have terribly bad habits, at least none that I know of. It's just that . . . . ."

"That?"

"I was scared, Dutch, more scared in a way than I was out in that woods. Maybe I still am, a little. I can't go through something like that again, and I'm afraid of another bad choice."

"I'm not a bad choice, Pat," he said softly.

"I know that."

"Why do you know that now and you didn't before?"

"I wasn't sure when I saw your van, but I knew it the moment I heard your voice in those woods and knew you were on our trail. I knew we'd be all right and that you would get us out of it. I knew then that I'd been really stupid. I was going to tell you about my past, but when I came over you told me about the offer and you were going to New York with Marcie I thought, . . well, you know what I thought. Anyway, now you know, and I'm sorry I was such an idiot about everything."

"And if you know I'm not a bad choice, what's the problem. Pat?" She gave him a faint smile. "Then let me rewind and say it again. I had a great time, Doc, and I'd like to do it again. How about it?"

"What about Marcie?"

"You want Marcie to come along on our date? That's a little weird, but I could ask her. Of course it's a long flight from New York just to be fifth wheel on a dinner date, but I can ask."

"She's staying in New York?"

"Yes. There's nothing for her to come back here for."

She leaned forward in her chair, her eyes searching his. "Nothing?"

He leaned forward, his face close to hers. "Nothing. And if you continue to sit like that, Doctor Stallings, I am going to seriously kiss you."

She continued to sit, *just* like that.

THE END